KANEN

SEALs of Honor, Book 20

Dale Mayer

Books in This Series:

KANEN: SEALS OF HONOR, BOOK 20
Dale Mayer
Valley Publishing

Copyright © 2019

ISBN-13: 978-1-773361-16-1
Print Edition

About This Book

His best friend's wife is in trouble...

A panicked phone call sends Kanen flying across the ocean to find that she's been held captive in her apartment, tortured for something her dead husband supposedly hid.

Only she knows nothing about it and her husband is, well, dead...

Dead men don't talk – or do they? As they unravel the mystery Kanen has to delve into his friend's life to see what he'd done that put his wife in jeopardy. And find her captor, before he decides to kill her.

Laysa doesn't know what this man wants, but after seeing Kanen again after so long she knows what she wants. But is it a betrayal of her husband? Then why was her husband hiding things?

And why did her captor want them? Even worse, if he got them in his possession, what was he planning to do with them?

COMPLIMENTARY DOWNLOAD

DOWNLOAD a *complimentary* copy of TUESDAY'S CHILD? Just tell me where to send it!

http://dalemayer.com/starterlibrarytc/

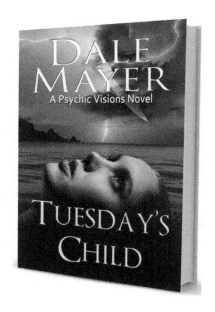

CHAPTER 1

NOT LONG AFTER the nightmare for Deli and Jackson had begun with a local training op and then had ended on base, several of the guys from their tight-knit units, plus their girlfriends, had gathered together to enjoy part of their days off. It wasn't odd to see them on a Tuesday, relaxing in the early evening hours, catching some downtime when they could. Kanen Larson studied Deli and Jackson, cuddling on the couch, wondering how Mason's magic could have spread for so long and so far. Kanen was happy for his friend. Hell, Kanen was surrounded by men so damn blissfully happy that it was almost enough to make a guy sick. Most of those lucky guys and gals had migrated outside to the barbecue pit, cleaning off the grill, readying it for the next time, helping themselves to more cold beers in the coolers.

But Kanen wasn't jealous—that wasn't part of who he was. Maybe envious. He wouldn't mind finding his soul mate. But it wasn't why he was here. It wasn't why he was friends with all these men. They were good men—the kind to call on when in trouble. The best kind of men to spend time with, whether at work or when time to play. Kanen was blessed, and he knew it. These were great guys. And the women they'd met? ... Wow, they were something else. Talk about raising the bar.

Mason had started everyone down a path where they

were all helpless to do anything but follow. And the thing was, not one of them seemed to mind.

Jackson looked at Kanen and raised an eyebrow.

Kanen just shrugged. "You two look good together."

Jackson smiled, wrapped his arm around Deli's shoulder and hugged her close. "Feels good together too," he admitted.

Kanen's phone pinged. A reminder alarm that he didn't need to read. He grabbed his go-bag and waved goodbye. "I'm off to Germany for training."

Jackson shook his head. "I hear you'll be doing night maneuvers in the Alps. And I'm missing out on that."

"Next time," Kanen said and left the latest lovebirds alone.

EVEN WITH A navy transport, the transatlantic flight took fourteen hours transit time plus added another nine hours, due to Germany's time zone compared to San Diego's. Meaning, Kanen spent most of Wednesday airborne.

No problem. He had gotten reacquainted with Taylor and had met Nelson for the first time. All the guys from various navy units gathered together here and had been encouraged to sleep on the transport, so they would be alert for nighttime maneuvers. Kanen had done that. Otherwise he had read the specs on the newest of the new equipment he would be trying out, from rappelling gear to night-vision scopes to bulletproof vests to small and large artillery to new freeze-dried food options, and whatever else they had assembled for SEAL approval or further input.

The transport arrived somewhere in the south of Germany at about 7:30 p.m., with the SEALs ordered to set up camp and to return to the transport on the double for their first night of four consecutive nights of training. Tonight Kanen and the others would be dropped in an undisclosed location well after dusk, picked up at midnight—and later each successive day—said pickup location given to them in code this time.

"Testing our code-breaking abilities early, I see," Taylor noted.

Nelson laughed, slapped him on the back. "Good times."

Kanen smiled, already enjoying how well he worked with these guys.

He was still smiling when he boarded the transport right at midnight, along with Taylor and Nelson. "Some of our toys tonight were unbelievable," Kanen said. "And the nighttime view of the Bavarian Alps was unbelievable."

"No kidding," Taylor said. "And they have surprises for us on that final night."

Nelson nodded. "Heard it was to test our learning curves."

"Should be interesting," Kanen said, still smiling.

MORNING QUICKLY FOLLOWED, now a Thursday. Just to mix things up, they were woken up early, dropped into an undisclosed area and expected to run a ten-mile jaunt with their sixty-pound packs back to their camp, using their wits and geographical markers. Then, once more, the transport took them to one of Germany's lakes, where they swam five miles in sixty-degree temperatures. Luckily they wore new thermal wetsuits that worked surprising well to keep their body temperatures near normal.

They heard murmurs that some extended sunset and sunrise excursions were planned to see if these new and improved wetsuits hid any thermal readings past those times of day. If so, more daytime maneuvers would be scheduled to further test that theory.

Then the guys were transported back to camp, where they were told to crash until needed again.

As soon as Kanen reached his sleeping bag, his eyes closed, and he fell deep into sleep.

He got two hours of sleep and was again on the transport. He and the others were dropped off at the foot of a mountain right at dusk on Thursday evening and were told to hike up to the first mountain camp they found. Without a map. This peak was deceptive. It may have been lower than the surrounding mountains, but its slope contained mostly rocks waiting to slide off the mountain and down, all aided by gravity and their own body weight.

Tonight the transport would pick them up at the base of the mountain at 1:00 a.m., providing they checked in at the first mountain camp beforehand. Groups of three were to hike together. Kanen was joined by Nelson and Taylor.

"More fun and games in the navy," Nelson joked.

The guys all laughed and strapped on their packs and took off at a good clip, determined to make the best time of the whole exercise.

One hour into their mountain trek, Kanen's cell phone rang.

He pulled it out, checked the time—8:04 p.m.—and saw it was his friend Laysa, calling from England, making it 7:05 p.m. her time. He waggled his cell phone to his buddies. "We're still getting cell phone reception. Must not be high enough yet to need the sat phone." He lifted the phone to his ear and cheerfully called out, "How is Laysa doing? Trying to whip all those little students into shape, making them sit up and pay attention?" he teased.

A broken sob was his only answer.

He straightened. "Laysa, what's wrong?"

Another sob, then an attempt to speak. But nothing came out.

"Take it easy. It's all right. I'm here. What's the matter?"

Her voice broke as she whispered, "Kanen."

"Yes, it's me," he said. "What's the matter? Talk to me. ... What's the problem?"

Taylor stared at Kanen, a frown line forming between his eyebrows.

Nelson perked up too.

Kanen shrugged, not sure what was going on yet. What he did know was Laysa didn't get upset over the little things. He paced about in a semi-level spot about three feet by three feet. "Laysa, talk to me," he urged. "What's happening?"

She cried out again—her tone raspy, as if she'd been crying a lot. And it was a tone he recognized. Her husband had been one of his best friends since forever. Since Blake's death almost a year ago, Kanen and Laysa had talked all the time, and her voice, at least in the beginning, had been tear soaked then too. But he'd never heard her like this.

"Tell me what's going on," he urged quietly. "I can't help you if you don't tell me."

Suddenly she shrieked in terror, then sobbed.

"Laysa," he yelled. "What's happening?"

A stranger spoke, his voice deadly. "Laysa can't talk right now. If you want to see her alive again, I suggest you listen."

Kanen's heart froze. His chest seized. What the hell? He spun to look at Taylor, who even now stood with his hands planted on his hips over a wide stance, ready to jump in and help. And he didn't yet have a clue what was going on either.

"Who is this?" Kanen barked. "What did you do to Laysa?"

"Did you hear me?" the stranger mocked. "Listen to me and do exactly what you're told to do."

"What do you want? If you hurt Laysa, I swear to God, I'll hunt you down like the dog you are," Kanen growled.

"Nice thought. But that won't really work for me."

"You have no reason to hurt her. Laysa wouldn't hurt a fly."

"No, she probably wouldn't," the stranger said with a casual indifference. "But you, on the other hand, *Kanen*, would do a lot to save her."

Kanen stared at the phone. He put it on Speaker and held it out between him, Nelson and Taylor, all three hovering over it. "How do you know who I am?"

"Oh, I know a lot about you. You think you're better than everybody else—an asshole SEAL. But Laysa's husband never made the grade, did he? He was just a lowly seaman."

"He was a naval officer," Kanen growled. "He was proud to be who he was."

"But he wanted to be a SEAL with you," the stranger said mockingly. "Of course you didn't stay behind with him, and he couldn't stand up with you, so you moved on ahead of him. Then he bailed as soon as his tour was up. He couldn't cut the navy, could he?"

"What's this all about?" Kanen asked, trying to calm down. That earlier shriek Laysa had let loose had chilled Kanen to the bone. It was obvious she was in bigger trouble than any inkling he currently had. "What's this got to do with Laysa?"

"Blake has something of mine. And I want it back," the stranger said thoughtfully. "I wonder if he planned to keep it—without my permission."

"Impossible. Blake was a good man and a great friend," Kanen said. "Besides, he died almost a year ago. Whatever he knew died with him."

Taylor stared at Kanen with a question in his eyes, but Kanen had no clue who he was talking to. Regardless Kanen cared about Laysa. This asshole who held her was already in deep shit. He just didn't know it yet.

"Blake has my insurance policy," the stranger said on a harsh laugh. "So, if you want to see Laysa still breathing, you'll come and find that item Blake was holding for me. Maybe he gave it to you?"

"What is it I'm looking for?" Kanen asked cautiously.

"Oh, no, no. It's not that easy," Dead Man Walking said. "Needless to say, you'd recognize it if you saw it. Laysa says she has no idea what I'm talking about. So I thought maybe Blake gave it to his best friend. But, of course, you won't give me what I want without a little persuasion. I'm sure holding Laysa will encourage your cooperation."

Taylor leaned in closer to the phone.

"I don't know what you're talking about," Kanen said, his mind sorting through his options. "Blake didn't give me anything to hold for him. I hadn't even spoken to him in the weeks before his death, much less seen him."

"Well, that's too bad for you and Laysa then, isn't it?" the stranger continued in a conversational tone. "Because, if you don't bring me what I want—and soon—dear Laysa will pay the consequences. The countdown clock is ticking."

The phone went dead.

CHAPTER 2

"**W**HAT THE HELL is going on over there?" Kanen asked. "I need to bug out. If I can't talk Mason into the transport dropping me off near London, then I'm on the next commercial flight."

"I didn't know Blake. What was he like?"

Kanen turned on Taylor. "He was a good guy," he said defensively. "He'd never have done anything illegal—not knowingly."

"I didn't say he would have," Taylor said calmly, holding out a hand, palm up. "But remember that we don't know everyone the way we think we do, and we can't be sure what was going on in Blake's life at the time of his death."

"I'd swear on my honor that Blake would never have done anything criminal."

"It doesn't have to be criminal," Nelson said quietly, facing the two of them. "A friend may have asked him to hold something. Or gave him something innocently, without Blake realizing it was important. Like a code or a key to a safe-deposit box or something like that."

"We need to wrap our heads around the fact that," Kanen said, "Laysa apparently is being held against her will, beaten for information she doesn't have, and her captor is damn short on patience."

"You care about this woman?" Nelson asked.

Kanen ran his hand through his hair. "I've known her for decades. We were all friends growing up together. She ended up marrying Blake. They were happy," he admitted. "I've become closer to her since Blake's death but as a friend. She just needed to know somebody was there for her after Blake was gone."

"That's huge," Nelson said. "Losing anyone is terrible—but a spouse? ... That's got to be a special kind of terrible. She must appreciate that you helped her through that."

Kanen hoped he had been of some solace to her, but, right now, his mind was caught on something else. "Did that asshole go through her Contacts list and find me, or did he already know who I was?"

"Or she told him," Nelson said. "I'll play devil's advocate here for a moment. Can you trust her? Do you believe she would be a part of this? That maybe she herself is looking for something Blake left behind?"

Kanen stared at Nelson blankly as Laysa's cries still rang in his ears. No way was that terror faked. "No. You'd have to meet her to understand. She's a lot of things, but a liar, thief or just plain petty? No, she's not any of those."

Nelson and Taylor looked at Kanen for a long moment, as if trying to read the truth in his face. Then they both gave nods.

Now that they believed him, Kanen let a *whoosh* from his chest. He sat down on the bare cold ground as he dialed Mason's number. When he heard Mason on the line, Kanen explained the situation.

"Location?"

"Ipswich, England."

"How long has she been there?"

He racked his brain, trying to think. "Four years maybe."

"Who does she work for?"

"A preschool. Can't remember the name," he said.

"When did Blake die?"

"September ninth of last year." His tone turned dark. "He was in a car accident."

"Was it caused by another person?"

Kanen froze. He slowly turned away when he answered, as if Taylor and Nelson couldn't still hear his side of the conversation. "No, the police said it was an accident. He ran off a cliff. Possibly avoiding some debris in the road or maybe an animal."

Silence followed.

Then Mason asked in a soft voice, "Do you still believe that?"

"Shit." Kanen tried to think, but his mind wouldn't obey his orders. "At the time it seemed strange because he was one of the better drivers I've ever known. He loved speed, and he used to race cars. That was one of his hobbies. He was hoping to have his own race car someday. He was a pro at the wheel."

"He still could have been going too fast, taking a corner too quickly," Mason said calmly. "That doesn't mean anybody else was involved."

"I know. Yet," Kanen said, his free hand fisted, "I don't know what to believe now."

"You can deal with that later. Right now, I can contact some people in England. I'll get back to you in five." Mason hung up.

Kanen stared at the blank screen on his phone and then checked on flights to Ipswich or London or wherever would get him to Laysa the fastest. By the time he had the data he needed, Mason called.

"MI6 will be waiting for you, no matter where you land."

"*Great.*" Kanen gave a harsh laugh.

"Yeah, they aren't happy to hear one of ours is coming to town either," Mason said. "You know we can't do much from this end without their knowledge."

"You could ask them to assist us instead of hindering us at every turn," Kanen said. "Blake was a former US naval officer with an honorable discharge. I don't care if somebody from NCIS joins me or one of our own unit, but I have to go."

"How early can you get there?"

"If I go commercial, I won't land until sometime after ten tomorrow morning."

"I've got time off coming," Nelson said.

Taylor spoke up too. "Me too. I'm coming with you."

Mason's voice came loud and clear through the phone. "Hold on to that thought, guys. I'll call back in a moment." And once again he hung up.

Kanen addressed Taylor and Nelson. "I'd love to have you two join me, if Mason can afford to cut all three of us loose at once. I don't need an entire team. It'd be nice to have at least one guy for backup. Two would be great." Kanen's phone pinged with an incoming text.

Formal request coming from the US government to MI6, asking for their assistance.

A second text read **Don't book any flights yet.**

Kanen grinned. "Mason doesn't want any flights booked at this time. What do you bet Mason snagged the navy transport for us?" Kanen heard another *ping* on his phone, a text update. **Transport on stand-by for you. Working out**

logistics. Will call with names of your team in five. With confirmed pickup time in next text or two.

Kanen nodded and waited to hear who would be going with him.

When Mason called back, he said, "Okay, I've got Nelson joining you for sure. Among his other skills, he'll be especially good for logistics, having spent a lot of time in England. I need to lock down another, someone with some techie leanings too. I'm hoping it will be Taylor, since he's with you as well and has already volunteered." And Mason was gone.

"Nelson, you're approved for this technically off-duty mission. Thanks for lending your expertise. I'm all for it," Kanen said. "Taylor, you're next in line for approval." Then Kanen frowned. "Even if we get the transport, when will they pick us up?"

Taylor shook his head. Nelson gave a one-shoulder shrug.

Kanen snorted. "We're farther than we should be for being only an hour out. Let's head back, double-time, see if we can reach the base of this mountain at top speed without incurring any injuries."

After about a mile of sideways jogging down the mountain, Kanen stopped.

The others did too, staring at him.

"I think I should contact Charles."

Nelson frowned. "Don't know Charles."

"Charles is in the underground line of our work, helps us out when we're overseas," Taylor explained to Nelson, then turned to Kanen. "Maybe wait for Mason to let you know if you're going as a civilian or as a SEAL. If this will be as official visit, then it's hotels all the way. Otherwise, Charles should have the space."

Nelson added, "Ipswich is only like seventy-five miles from London. But, if Charles resides in the capital city, we'd be closer to Laysa if we book into a local Ipswich hotel."

"As long as it happens now, I'm good. Maybe on the navy transport, I can sneak into the country. That way, this asshole can't track me. At least not initially. Might give me some time to sneak up on him."

Taylor grimaced. "If he's a professional hacker, he'll know, transport or commercial. He may have a source in MI6 who'll give you away. I figure Laysa's captor will somehow have immediate notification when you arrive in the country."

"And, if he's such a pro, he'll get into all the databases he needs." Kanen snorted. "Hell, it's probably even easier to do now than it was before."

"Either way," Taylor continued, "we must assume he will know before you enter the country, finding your flight info or whatever. If booking a hotel, make it look like you arrived, then sneak out, in case somebody is waiting for you."

Kanen swore. "Right. Even if I just switch rooms, that could help me lose anybody on my tail."

"Now you're thinking. Plus Charles is a great source of all things that you might need for supplies," Taylor said in a low voice, raising one eyebrow in way of question. "You can always contact him after you speak to Mason."

Kanen understood. He'd never met Charles, but Kanen knew lots of guys who had. Mostly men who worked for Levi. And everybody by now knew who Levi was and the team of ex-military he'd amassed around him. Kanen had spoken to Charles over the years; Kanen just hadn't met him in person. And, as much as he understood Taylor's suggestion to wait for Mason to get back to him, Kanen wanted to give Charles a heads-up. If for no other reason than to clear that To Do item off his mental list and to establish his local contact person. Plus, Kanen couldn't traipse down this mountain and text at the same time.

He tapped his finger on his phone for a long moment, then typed a text to Charles, saying Kanen was in trouble and would arrive no later than tomorrow morning.

The response came back in less than a minute. **I'm always here for you**.

"Maybe double- or triple-book those hotel rooms," Nelson suggested, "to delay that asshole a bit from finding you."

Kanen heard Nelson, but, inside his head, Kanen was numb. He kept glancing at his watch, imagining how scared Laysa must be, how much pain she was in, what the asshole was doing to her and who the hell he was.

WHO THE HELL is this asshole? Laysa asked herself, yet again. He had been hysterical for the last couple hours. He had beat her first, asked questions afterward. But all of it was insensate nonsense. He seemed to be calming down a bit, if only because he got sidetracked by terrorizing Kanen for a bit on the phone.

He wore a black full-face knit ski mask, a muscle shirt and jeans, his jacket on the couch, with a suspicious gun-shaped bulge in one of its pockets. That she couldn't see his face she'd taken great comfort in, thinking, if she couldn't identify him, then maybe he wasn't planning on killing her.

Now she wasn't so sure. His jerky mannerisms made her afraid he had a bullet with her name on it. Not with that rage he couldn't contain. Her body ached; she was already bruised from his initial blows. Although most had been centered on her torso, her jaw would bloom nicely soon.

That he'd pulled Kanen into this made it even worse. She doubted her friend knew any more than she did. She had a simple flat in Ipswich, where she'd lived with Blake. But she'd removed most of his personal items at this point. Kanen had helped clear out much of Blake's things right after the funeral, as it hurt her too much to see them. She had even boxed up more personal items, but they had remained here, until she'd taken time later to go through them—Blake's letters and cards to her and other memorabilia. What if she had already disposed of this thing her captor wanted so badly, not realizing how important it was, like some key that wasn't familiar? What if she'd thrown it away?

Suddenly her captor looked around her apartment. He was not very tall for a man but lean and muscular. His arms showed ripped muscles. His hands were large, yet bony. He turned and looked at her. "Did you always live here with your husband?"

"Yes. Since we moved to England." She remained in the armchair in the far corner of the living room. Every time she tried to get up, he shoved her roughly back down again.

"Do you have a storage unit here?"

"Not here in the building," she said hesitantly, wondering at the look in his eyes, as if he were testing her. "One of those storage units at a yard full of them."

An odd light came into his gaze, confirming her suspicions. "Where is it?"

She frowned. "On Bellamy Street. But I don't remember the exact address. It's one of those big-name storage companies with rows of units."

"What number is your unit?"

"One-thirteen."

"Is it locked?"

She nodded mutely.

"Where's the key?"

"In the kitchen junk drawer," she said.

He walked into her small galley kitchen. She could hear him opening and closing drawers. And then he walked toward her, shaking the container, the keys rattling inside. He held it out. "Which one is it?"

She took the container, stirred around the key mess. Spying the little silver key, she picked it up. The spare was on her key ring. She handed this one to him. "This is it."

He studied her for a long moment, checked his watch, then said, "Stand up. We're going for a ride."

She stared at him, but she couldn't move. He took a menacing step forward.

"What's the matter, bitch? Didn't you hear me?"

"Leave me here," she said in anger. "I've done everything you've asked. Just leave me here when you go look at the stuff."

He shook his head. "No, it could be a trick."

"Like I knew beforehand that you would break into my home before I returned from work? That you would beat me up today, not tomorrow? Like I knew Blake had your stuff? Besides, what could I possibly gain by tricking you? Tie me up if you want. Just leave me alone and go check the storage unit."

He stood for a long moment, as if weighing the pros and cons of leaving her tied up and alone versus taking her where she could possibly escape or attract attention. Then he gave a clipped nod. "I'll do that. And thanks for the idea to tie you up."

He disappeared into the kitchen and returned with the packages of straps she'd forgotten were there. She groaned when she saw them. "Please, not tight."

He zip-tied her legs, one to each of the legs of the chair. And then her arms behind her. He glanced at his watch again, key in hand, and said, "I'll be back in two hours." He narrowed his gaze at her. "Make sure you're here." He turned and left.

CHAPTER 3

THE DOOR SLAMMED shut in front of her. Everything hurt, but she ignored the pain. She had two hours. He'd be back, and she'd be in deeper trouble than she already was. She twisted her fingers, trying to loosen one of her hands from the zip strap behind her. He'd pulled the strap tight, but she had balled up her hands into fists, trying to bulk up her wrists. It worked slightly, in that she had gained a little wiggle room within the tie.

Laysa continued to work her fingers until she got one hand through, then the second to slide out. Immediately she pulled her arms forward and rubbed her sore wrists. She rotated her shoulders, groaning at the pain from just being tied up that short amount of time. Both of her feet were strapped to the legs of the chair. They would be harder to release. The coffee table was beside her. She opened the drawer beneath it, hoping for something sharp. But, no, there was nothing.

She straightened up, and, holding the chair, she hobbled and hopped her way to the kitchen. Soon she had the zips cut. She replaced the chair where it had been. Grabbing her wallet and her phone, she took one last look around her small apartment and slipped into the hall. Afraid her tormenter would be standing outside the building, waiting for her, watching for her, she raced upstairs instead of down.

One floor up, she knocked on Carl's door. He was a friend, but he also was a cop. When he opened it, she bolted in. "Close the door," she whispered softly from the living room. "Hurry, shut it."

When he did, he turned and looked at her.

His wife, Sicily, hopped up and asked, "What's the matter, Laysa? Oh, my God! Are you hurt?" When Laysa choked up with tears and couldn't respond, Sicily added, "I'll get you an ice pack for your face."

Laysa gasped and sobbed, partly in relief at getting free but also because she knew the guy would be back. She explained what had happened, taking the ice pack from Sicily with a small smile.

Carl was on the phone immediately, bringing in a team.

"Send somebody to the storage unit address I gave him," she said. "He'll be there. He should be there now."

"They will send someone," Carl said, then turned slightly to talk into the phone.

She glanced at her watch and nodded. "He's been gone at least fifteen minutes. He could be there already." She looked up at Carl. "Unless he knows I lied. I told him the correct general location. I just didn't tell him the right number for the storage unit. And I don't know why, but asking about this seemed like a trick question, or maybe he already knew about the storage unit. I don't know. ... Nothing there is worth worrying about. But, ... well, they are Blake's things. I don't want a stranger touching them. If he knows I lied, maybe he wanted to follow me to see who I trusted?"

Carl said, "It doesn't matter if he did. We'll get him. Keep that ice on your jaw."

Sicily patted the vacant seat near her and had Laysa sit

on the couch beside her. "I'm so sorry. That must have been terrifying."

Laysa nodded. She fumbled with her phone. "I have to tell Kanen that I'm safe."

"Why would that stranger think Kanen would have something or would know more?" Carl asked. "Were Kanen and Blake best friends?"

Laysa nodded. "We've all been friends for a long time, but Kanen lives in California." She held the phone to her ear. It rang, but there was no answer. Frustrated, she hit the Off button, wondering why it hadn't at least gone to voice mail. She redialed and waited. After ten rings, the voice mail kicked in. "Kanen, it's me, Laysa. I escaped. He will be looking for you. Don't come here. Keep yourself safe. I'll hide until the police capture him." Then she hung up.

She looked at Sicily. "I'm still shaking so badly." She held up her hand, and, indeed, the tremors made it difficult for her to hold the phone steady.

"Of course you are, my dear. Of course you are." Sicily stood. "Let me get you a cup of tea. That'll help."

Carl returned after finishing his phone call. "Let me get some photos," he said. When she balked, he added, "We need them for evidence." He brought out his phone and then stopped, looking at her. "I have to ask, did he hurt you further? Did he rape you?"

She pulled the ice away from her face and shook her head violently. "Thankfully, no. He beat me up pretty good though," she said, reaching to her swollen cheek and jaw. Now that she was safe, Laysa was more aware of her throbbing body. "I'm sure I'll be black and blue everywhere tomorrow."

He nodded. "After your tea, I'll take you to the hospital,

and we'll grab any evidence we can from you."

She winced. "You mean, like hairs or fibers?"

"Did you scratch him?"

She frowned, looking at her nails. "I certainly fought. I clawed at his muscle shirt. I don't know if any DNA is under my nails or not. I did get a good slug into his shoulder or back, but I think it was just my fist, no claws involved. He was wily, staying just far enough away, except for when he hit me."

"That may be," Carl said, "but we have to try."

She nodded but didn't hold out much hope.

Sicily returned with the tea. "It's not superhot. I wanted you to get some of it down fast."

Laysa sagged farther into the couch, her mind spinning in fear. "I feel like I need to get out of this building," she whispered. "I'm afraid you guys will be his victims too. I shouldn't have come." The more she sat here, the more worried she got. She slugged back several big sips of tea, put down the cup along with her ice pack and then bolted to her feet. "I can't stay," she cried out frantically. "He'll be back. He'll try to find me, and he said he'd kill me if I wasn't there when he returned."

Carl reached out and grabbed her. "Easy. I'll take you to the hospital myself."

She stared at him, loving the friendship and the stability he represented in her world gone crazy. "I don't know," she whispered. "This guy is really good. Like, seriously good. For all I know, he's a pro, and I might be putting you in extreme danger." She looked at the front door, then looked at them. Red flags popped up all over in her mind. "I have to go. *Now.*"

She bolted for the front door. She couldn't understand

her panic, but it rode her hard. Just as she reached the top of the stairs, she saw somebody coming up the stairwell from below. It was *him*. Now she knew why she was so terrified. He'd found her Contacts info for Carl and Sicily on her phone. Her attacker was coming up here after them.

She raced back to the apartment and motioned to Carl, then whispered, "He's coming. He's coming. He's coming."

Carl slammed the door, locked the chain on top and called the security office in the apartment building.

She curled up in the far corner of the living room behind the couch, shaking violently, her arms wrapped around her knees, her mind spinning, uselessly trying to figure out what she was supposed to do.

Sicily bent in front of Laysa, holding her hands. "Whatever it is, we can do this," she whispered.

"What if he kills you?" Laysa asked painfully. "I'll never forgive myself. Coming to you for help has brought him to you."

Carl asked from the other side of the couch, "Did he see you?"

"I don't think so," she said, "but he would have heard the door, I'm sure."

"That doesn't mean he knows it was you though," Sicily said quietly.

Just then a hard sound came; wood shattered, and a bullet careened through the front door to land in the opposite wall.

Laysa gave a broken laugh and whispered, "Well, that answers that question."

Carl patted her hand, and she realized he was armed too. She stared at the gun in relief. "I didn't know you were allowed to have guns at home."

He shrugged. "Marksmanship is also a hobby. I do have licenses for them."

"As long as they shoot real bullets," she said, "I don't care if you have licenses or not. I just don't want to be taken by him again."

Carl waited. She watched, worried he was too old for this young, fit madman. But Carl stayed well out of the way and waited. No second bullet came. Nothing. Not a sound. Carl leaned over the corner of the couch, as if to assess the doorway.

Laysa whispered, "Don't go out there."

He looked at her and then shrugged.

She shook her head. "He'll be waiting."

"The cops should be here soon," Sicily whispered.

Laysa wasn't so sure. It seemed like the cops were slow everywhere. But then again, Carl was one of their own. Maybe he commanded a faster response than other people.

Just then her phone rang. She tried to shut it down but realized it was Kanen. Keeping her voice low, she whispered, "Hello?"

"What the hell happened?"

Quietly she explained what happened and where she was.

"And the police are on their way? Tell me they will handle this right now," he asked, his voice rising.

"Yes, that's what Carl said." She realized she'd forgotten to tell Kanen about him. "Carl is a cop."

"Good. I'm on my way to Ipswich. I should be at your apartment building in a few hours."

"No, no, no, no. You can't come."

He snickered. "Too bad. Two more guys are with me."

She shook her head. "You have to look after yourself.

He's after me and *you* now. When you come, he'll capture you too."

"Let him try," Kanen said, his voice hard, rough. "He'll pay for hurting you." There was silence, and then he asked, "Are you okay?"

She sighed. "I'm fine. He didn't rape me. He didn't really hurt me too badly, considering he could have killed me. Carl wants me to go to the hospital and get examined and have the hospital do a forensic something or other." She was still so shocked that her words completely escaped her. "To make sure they collect any evidence there might be."

"I agree. Make sure you're never alone. If you need security until I get there, then you let me know. I'll have somebody by your side."

"No. No, it'll be fine. I can get Carl's help too," she said. Now that she was free, she was sorry Kanen was involved. It had put him in terrible danger.

"Don't ever try to stop me from coming to help or ever be afraid of calling me," he said sharply. "Our friendship goes too far back for that."

She smiled tremulously. "I was just thinking that. But thank you. I need this guy caught. I want this over with."

"I'm sure he's gone," Kanen said reassuringly. "But he won't have gone far. Be extra careful."

"Will do." Outside she could hear sirens approaching. "That's the police now," she said, starting to relax. "If he wasn't gone before, he will be now."

"Good. I'll call you as soon as I land." He hung up.

She cradled the phone against her chest, buried her face in her knees and waited. Sure enough she could hear shouts as the police entered the building and raced toward them.

Carl never moved. When a hard knock came on the

door, he called out, "Identify yourself." The constable replied with his name and number, then asking, "Are you Investigating Officer Carl McMaster?"

Instead of answering, Carl rose and opened the door. "I am. Come on in."

Six men entered, their weapons drawn. They thoroughly searched the apartment, and then two stayed while the other four continued to search the building.

Laysa's captivity was really over.

Taylor's a go. Transport's on another exercise. Available at 1:00 a.m. as planned. To take you wherever you want to go.

"Damn," Kanen said, showing the text to Nelson and Taylor.

"Not to mention," Nelson said, "we could have beat everybody's time on this molehill tonight."

Kanen slapped his newest SEAL buddy on the back. "Thanks, man. Glad you're coming with us."

LANDING THE NAVAL transport took special clearance. Kanen winced at that. *Our hacker asshole will note this special clearance.* At 4:00 a.m. on the dot, UK time, Kanen strode through customs and headed straight outside, ever alert. The minute he was free and clear from the crowds, he called Laysa. Her sleepy voice answered the phone, and he winced. "Sorry to wake you," he said gently. "It's your nighttime here. I just needed to make sure you were okay."

"I'm okay," she whispered. "I spent hours at the hospital, but I'm home now. Well, I'm in Carl's spare bedroom, not my own apartment."

"Good," Kanen said. "I'm walking out of the airport now. I'll be at my hotel soon."

"Why?" she wailed softly. "He'll come after you. You know that, right?"

"Like I said, he's welcome to try. I'll be waiting and watching for him." Kanen's voice was harsh. "If he wants a piece of me, that's good because I want a piece of him. Go back to sleep. I'll call you in a couple hours." Not giving her a chance to argue, he shut off the call and pocketed his phone.

Even at this ungodly hour, he caught sight of three guys in suits—MI6—spread about along the well-lit front of the airport, near the departing vehicles. One gave a gentle tap of his watch, without ever locking gazes with Kanen. He responded by tilting his chin upward ever-so-slightly, as if to say, *Message received.* The watch tap either meant MI6 was watching Kanen or how MI6 would catch up with him later. Or possibly both.

As expected, a shuttle waited for Kanen, and the two men he had traveled with converged here, each giving a subtle headshake. Granted, they had no facial description on this asshole—and he could have sent in any number of lookouts—but the guys didn't see any suspicious-looking characters in their brief tour of the airport. No one seemed particularly interested in them. No one followed them. Nelson had made a side trip to an out-of-the-way men's room, while Taylor had gone to baggage claim, despite all three men only having carry-on luggage.

The trio got into the back of the shuttle vehicle. The twenty-minute ride to the hotel was just enough time for the men to get acquainted with their new surroundings. Upon arrival at the hotel, Kanen registered and asked for a rental car to be available as soon as possible—a particularly nice perk with this hotel. The front desk manager explained the car keys would be here within the hour, Kanen grabbed his bags, nodded his thanks and headed for the stairs. The three walked to the second floor. Checking that no one watched, they entered through their door and headed straight for the adjoining suite via a hidden connecting door. Charles had recommended this hotel specifically for that reason and the rental car availability.

Kanen's phone pinged. He checked his alert, shaking his head. "That asshole never sleeps. He's already made us as checked in here."

"So he's a hacker," Taylor suggested.

"Or," Nelson added, "he paid a cabbie to loop around the block until the three of us arrived via the airport shuttle."

Kanen shrugged. "*Or* he could have paid the front desk employee to send him a physical signal or a text." Kanen stared at his phone, then addressed the guys. "I don't think he'll make an appearance this soon. Or ever. He's a bully, hitting women. Doubt he'd attack one SEAL, much less three. But … my money's on him being a hacker, tracking our every move."

In the adjoining suite, with the disappearing door closed and locked, they set up a command center and connected a video chat to their US contact and to Charles in England. Charles's face came on the video. It was really early here, still dark outside, but, according to Ice, Charles always looked dapper and friendly.

"Hello, young man," Charles said with a smile. "Nice to see you again too, Mason."

Mason acknowledged he was available to help any fellow

SEAL abroad.

"I don't think I've seen you face-to-face before, Kanen," Charles noted.

Kanen grinned at him. "No, you haven't. But we've talked."

"There's a first time for everything. I hear you have trouble knocking on your door."

Kanen nodded. "Laysa is now in trouble. Apparently her captor gave Blake something to hold for him. Now the asshole wants it back, but Laysa doesn't know anything about it. Neither do I."

"And neither of you have anything that you're aware of, correct?"

Kanen nodded. "It's not like Blake sent me a parcel before he died, asking me to hold on to it in case anything happened to him."

"We're assuming that's what happened to Blake himself, correct? That somebody did hand him this package and told him to hang on to it for a few minutes, a few months, a lifetime?"

"As close as we can figure from Laysa's assailant's words, yes," Kanen said. "But Blake may have thought it was completely innocent. For all we know, Blake thought he was holding on to a package of mementos of the guy's former girlfriends or something."

"Right. And nothing has been said as to why her captor wants it now?"

"*The situation has changed*," Kanen paraphrased Laysa's earlier words. "Apparently he needs this for *insurance*. I did help put some of Blake's belongings into a storage unit after his funeral, and her captor headed for that unit, leaving her tied up. But it wouldn't take him long to figure out that, while the address was correct, the unit number was not."

"So she sent him to a storage facility but not to the right unit. Interesting," Charles said. "That almost makes it seem like she does know what he's talking about."

"No. You have to understand it from her point of view. She cleared out much of Blake's stuff immediately, finding it hard to keep so many memories around. We put some in the storage unit for her to deal with later, and some of the more personal items were boxed up but left at home, and lots we gave away. I doubt she even remembers what went where. Although she did say that she had been through most of Blake's personal items, putting his cards and letters to her in their picture album. I don't believe she has much still boxed up at home."

At that, Charles nodded slowly. "She's a very resourceful lady, even under duress." His face was drawn with another understanding. "That does make sense. I'm so sorry for her."

"I am too," Kanen said. "I've stayed in touch with her. We usually talk weekly. And lately she's been much better. We haven't needed to connect quite as often. She's a really good woman, and she was very much in love with Blake."

"So you helped her pack everything away?"

"I helped her move most of it to the storage unit. I didn't pack up anything. I did the heavy lifting. She packed the boxes."

"So you have no clue what was boxed and moved in the storage unit, much less what the assailant is looking for?"

"No. I didn't see anything unusual as she packed up Blake's things," Kanen said, "but obviously we have to go through the storage unit more carefully now to see what this guy is after."

"It could be as small as a CD or a USB," Charles said.

"That makes the unidentified item even more difficult to find."

"I know," Kanen said quietly. "If he's tech-savvy, a real hacker, the best way to handle that might be to set up a team at the storage facility itself. The cops did when Laysa escaped but found no sign of her assailant. We should check it again. And we'll slowly search through the storage items, careful to check out all electronics. I assume this *insurance* entails some sensitive data. So it would make sense that it's computer-oriented. But it could just as easily be paperwork."

"True," Charles said, looking away, then glanced back. "Do you have enough manpower? I could help with that."

"No, we're good," Kanen said. "I have two men with me. MI6 is not impressed we're here."

At that, Charles's face split into a wide knowing grin. "With good reason. They've dealt with a few other US Navy personnel, current and former, coming over and raising a bit of Cain."

"You're talking about Badger, aren't you? I heard through the grapevine how he and his team were here a couple times."

"I never had a chance to meet him myself," Charles said, laughing. "But anything that happens in Levi's world, I'm usually apprised of it, especially when it overflows into my own backyard."

"Too bad Badger didn't contact you," Kanen said. "You probably could have helped him out."

"I think we'll connect sometime in the near future," Charles said with a smile. "People like Badger have to go off as a lone ranger to deal with the emotions that drive them. And then they slowly realize how they aren't alone and that teams are required, and it helps a lot to have skillful and gifted men in your corner. Badger accomplished what he needed to, and, for that, I'm grateful. But I also know England is grateful too—that they left, that is."

Kanen laughed. "I take it a few dead bodies littered his visit."

Charles nodded. "MI6 contacted me back then to see if I knew anything about him. But Levi helped to explain that scenario."

Kanen sat back and smiled. "You know? The more I work in this field, the more I realize how interconnected we all are. Levi is no longer in the military, but he's doing just as much of a service for the world as anybody could possibly do. And Badger is the same. Plus, both remain close to Mason and his various navy teams."

"Not exactly sure what Badger is doing these days," Charles said. "I believe he has some contract work with Levi, and that would be good because, once you're a protector and a defender, it's very hard to turn off those traits. He'd probably drive his partner nuts if he wasn't involved in a similar line of work. Although I guess Kat is his wife now. I did get an invitation but couldn't make their wedding date."

"Yes, so I heard. He's a good man, and, from the bit of gossip I heard, that was one hell of a wedding." Kanen still chuckled as he disconnected his video call with Charles and Mason, then turned to see the guys had set up both audio and video in this room. At his nod, they slipped into the decoy room—where they were booked into for registration purposes—and set it up to look like they had been there, laying out a few pieces of clothing and some personal items, pulling back the covers and making it look like somebody had been sitting on the bed. They also set up more audio and video devices. With the bugs in place, the Do Not Disturb sign hanging outside on the doorknob and a single strand of hair on the door inside to show whether anyone entered this room, they slipped back over to the other side, closed the wall panel so it hid the connection to the next room, and relaxed.

Kanen glanced around and nodded. "This is perfect."

"Need a plan of action," Nelson said.

"We'll go to her apartment and to the storage unit," Kanen said, "and set up electronics with laptops at each place. That way we can open any USB keys and other devices we might find."

"Is there power at the storage unit?" Taylor asked.

Kanen nodded. "There is. I don't know exactly how much though. We'll need to bring a power bar and must be prepared to slip out and get more equipment, if need be. We'll be working in the dark, so as not to give away our position, and thus we have to plan in task lighting. We can't have the door open because this guy is looking for this particular unit. I don't know if he believed the information she gave him. It was the right address but the wrong storage unit."

"That was smart of Laysa to do that," Nelson noted.

Kanen nodded. "If our asshole has access online, or if he's any kind of a hacker, he might find out the names of the renters of the storage units as well. So he could locate Blake's locker without Laysa's help. Even a good sob story is likely to loosen the lips of whoever is in the office. We've seen it happen time and time again. Just because there are rules, that doesn't mean they aren't broken."

Taylor nodded. "We'll double-check that we have every-thing we need before we get there, so we can camp out and go through the place."

"What about letting Laysa know what we're doing?" Nelson asked.

Kanen hesitated. "She'd be pissed if we were doing this without her knowledge. She's kind of a control freak. Probably from her schoolteacher mentality. But we have to get this done regardless. I'm not sure what the appropriate answer is here."

"You should probably involve her," Nelson said.

Kanen shook his head. "Not sure I want to do that. She can be fairly obstinate when she puts her foot down."

"But still, it's her personal belongings," Nelson said. "Her *dead husband's* personal belongings."

Kanen nodded slowly. "Good point. Okay, so I'll tell her what we're doing and that I don't want her going to either place alone. Not until we've caught this asshole."

"He didn't find whatever it was while he was there in her apartment yesterday," Nelson said, "so ..."

"What are the chances he missed it?" Taylor asked.

"No way to know," Kanen said simply. "We don't know how big this *insurance policy* is or even *what* it is. But she has lived there for a while."

"It would be faster to search the apartment first, rather than a storage unit," Nelson said.

Kanen looked at him. "Probably, yes. While we were transported here, her place was full of police, taking fingerprints and checking for any DNA. I don't know that she'll sleep there ever again. Seems she was beaten up pretty good. At the moment, she's still in the apartment building, staying with the cop and his wife who she'd run to in the first place. That'll give her a certain amount of protection."

"Well, the cops should be done, so why don't we move on to her place and do a quick search ourselves?" Taylor asked.

Kanen thought about that and nodded. "That works. Her captor will be watching. We can count on that. It might lure him to us."

"That's a good thing," Nelson said. "We need to capture this guy before he tries to snag you next."

Kanen shook his head. "I would welcome that," he said. "What I don't want is him getting his hands on Laysa again. She's valiant, but she can only handle so much. She's had a tough year as it is. I don't want this to ruin her life, to sour her outlook on everything." Kanen checked his watch. "We could get in now, do a full search and get out. It's not yet sunrise."

The men jumped to their feet.

Kanen stood too. "Agreed. Let's do that first. And let's go now."

CHAPTER 4

LAYSA WOKE EARLY that morning. She reached for her cell phone, checking the time. It wasn't even five-thirty yet. She lay here for a long moment, wondering if she could go back to sleep. But, now that her body and mind were awake, all she could think about was getting up. She was normally an early riser, but she was in Carl's apartment and didn't feel she could get up and walk around freely.

She'd also left her laptop in Carl's living room and didn't have a change of clothes with her. She'd love nothing more than a hot bath and to get into clean clothes. Once her mind went from that topic to her apartment only one floor below, it wasn't a far stretch to wonder if she could safely go downstairs and grab a few personal belongings. Surely the police were done looking through her apartment? There wasn't any reason for them to take their time or to work through the night. Surely there were forensics to collect and photographs to take but not anything else to do, was there? She waited as long as she could, but the idea wouldn't leave her alone. Finally she got up, slipped on her bloodstained clothes and crept out to the main part of the apartment. As far as she could tell, Carl and his wife didn't wake up.

Laysa stared at the front door and frowned. Was she being a foolish? She didn't have any fear about going back down to her apartment, so her internal alarm was okay with this idea. It would be risky for her captor to return, even if he didn't have his insurance policy yet. After all, the police had been there probably late into the night. Feeling emboldened at the idea, she scribbled a quick note for Carl and put it on the couch, then walked out the front door, leaving it unlocked so she could return. She made her way quietly to the stairs. The night lights were still on up and down the hallway and in the stairwells.

But outside it was pitch-black. Normal people would be asleep at this time. But not her.

Standing before her apartment door, she used her key and entered. She found no sign of any security—a guard or a camera—or even crime-scene tape. Nothing here let her know if the police were done or if they would return. The place still looked as she'd last seen it, with the drawers dumped all over the place.

With her heart pounding, she took the first step back into her apartment, worried that maybe her captor could have come back around for her. It was a terrifying thought, but there was no reason for it.

Just her fear talking in her mind. At least that's what she told herself.

She headed toward her bedroom and turned on the light. She quickly grabbed an overnight bag and a couple changes of clothes. She didn't know how long she would be upstairs. Part of her wanted to stay among her own familiar surroundings and another part never wanted to return. All she needed was enough to get through the next day or two. She added a light sweater, and, as she zipped up her carry bag, she thought she heard something in the living room. She froze, rushed to the wall and turned off the light.

There she waited, her breath caught in her throat, just to

hear the sound again. She tried to calm down and to convince herself that it was probably something outside. But, in her heart, she knew somebody was in her apartment. And then she couldn't stop cursing herself for being such a fool.

Maybe her captor had been watching. Hell, maybe he had never left the building, and the police had somehow missed him.

Maybe he'd been waiting for somebody to return to the apartment, and, once he'd seen the light, he'd come in. Just the thought sent chills down her spine. She didn't know what to do. Her arms shook, and her stomach churned. She didn't dare get caught by that madman again. She didn't know if she should go in the bathroom, locking the door behind her, and wait, or could she exit the apartment without being seen?

The trouble was, she'd already given herself away by turning on the light.

Her only option was to make a run for it. Counting down in her mind—*three, two, one*—she bolted for the front door, swinging the bag behind her. She made no attempt to be quiet. Then she heard a mumbled shout behind her.

But that brought added speed to her heels. She hit the front door, her fingers scrabbling to grab the knob and to turn it in time to get out. As she was about to cross the threshold, arms grabbed her. She could hear someone calling to her, but she was too panicked to register anything, to understand who it was. Once she was grabbed, her mouth opened, and a hand clasped over her lips. She was dragged back inside.

Strong arms held her firmly. But he didn't move her toward the living room. He just held her tight. Somewhere through the dim panic in her mind, she thought she recognized his smell. She froze and then twisted her head and mumbled, "Kanen?"

He nodded, grinned and eased his grip.

She fully turned within his hold, threw her arms around his neck and clung to him. "Oh, my God! I thought it was *him* back again," She reared back and slugged him in the chest. "Why would you terrify me like that?" Tears welled up. "Do you have any idea how scared I was?"

There was only silence afterward.

Then she flung herself into his arms, her arms tightly around his neck a second time, and whispered, "I'm so sorry. I'm so sorry. I'm so sorry."

He just held her close. Then she heard his deep voice, whispering against her ear, "It's all right. I shocked you. I'm sorry."

She sagged against him and knew it would be okay. She pulled back, the tears burning in the corners of her eyes. "I overreacted," she whispered.

He smiled. "It's my fault for scaring you."

She grinned up at him. "And I'm delighted to see you and not that asshole."

He stepped back slightly, studying her a little more intently. "I can see the asshole's handiwork turning purple already on your chin. ... What the hell are you doing here?"

Two men stepped out from the living room. She froze. They weren't alone.

"They're with me," Kanen said quietly.

She sagged against him in relief. "Thank God for that."

He introduced her to Taylor and Nelson.

She smiled, reached out a hand and shook both men's hands, saying, "Thank you for coming to help."

"Speaking of which," Kanen said, closing the front door

and leading her into the living room. "Tell us why you're down here."

"I woke up really early and couldn't sleep," she confessed. "All I wanted was a hot bath and a fresh change of clothes. I figured the police went home for the night, so they wouldn't be pissed at me for being in here. They searched the building, and the assailant was gone, so I feel a little safer. They also checked the storage unit, but he was gone from there as well." She sighed. "I needed to change clothes."

Everyone seemed to relax at that.

She frowned at Kanen, noticing the change in his body language. "You don't really think I came here for any other reason, do you?"

"I couldn't figure out why you'd come here," he said. "When we entered the apartment, I thought I saw a light flicker out. And I thought maybe the intruder had come back for another look through, but I couldn't tell for sure. Until you bolted for the front door." He gave an admiring look. "I forgot you'd been the best sprinter around."

She sighed. "But I still wasn't fast enough. You caught me." At that, she grinned. "As I recall, you were always the best catcher in our group too."

He chuckled. "That's baseball. Whereas you were the track-and-field star." He nudged her toward the couch.

She sat down, Kanen standing before her, the others nearby. "Now maybe I should ask why you guys are here and how you got in?"

"Like you, we were hoping the police were done and gone," Nelson said. "We figured, if this guy was looking for something, we should start here and make sure it wasn't close by before we headed to the storage unit."

She raised both hands in frustration. "I've done nothing

but think about that damn *insurance policy*. I have no clue what he's talking about. But help yourself. He was dumping left, right and center, trying to find whatever it was. But he never would tell me. I don't know if it was paperwork or a USB stick," she snapped, her ire getting the better of her again. "Another thing is, I haven't even paid for the storage unit. There were no reminder bills. For all I know, the contents have been confiscated."

"Blake could have prepaid for a year though," Nelson said. "That's normal. Maybe he took care of it. But, just to be clear, you're giving us permission to search it, as well as this apartment?" Nelson's tone was neutral, but his gaze was watchful.

She turned toward him and nodded. "Please do."

He gave a clipped nod and disappeared into her bedroom. She winced. "I guess now things get really invasive, don't they?"

Kanen bent closer to give her a tiny shake. "It already has. The minute that guy violated your space, it became invasive. We're just trying to help."

She sagged in place. "I'm sorry." She rubbed her temples with her hands, loose strands of hair flying around her face. "Maybe I should go upstairs and back to bed."

"If you want to, yes, please do." Kanen straightened and pointed a thumb to the door.

She gave a half laugh. "Hell no, I don't want to. What I want to do is visit with you. It seems so long since I've seen you." She stood, opened her arms and wrapped them around his waist and held him close to her a long moment; then she stepped back. "Go do what you have to do. It'd probably be easier if I'm not here. Plus I should let Carl and Sicily know that I'm okay. And I really need that bath." She headed to the front door, grabbed her bag, then turned. "Text me when you're done, and I'll meet you."

He nodded. She opened the front door and walked back up to Carl's place.

KANEN WATCHED HER walk out the door. He followed her to the hallway and waited until she walked up the stairs. She texted him a moment later. **I'm safe inside. Go back to work.**

He gave a half laugh. She knew he'd waited and watched, worried over her. But they'd been friends a long time. Of course he was worried about her. Of course he wanted to make sure she was safe.

Back inside, Nelson stopped what he was doing to look up at Kanen.

Kanen closed the door behind him and said, "Now that she's gone, let's do as thorough a check as we can." And they went at it.

They checked in between cushions—even unzipped the cushions to check inside—then underneath the couch and the bed, behind photos, in the dressers, under the drawers, in the toilet, every nook and cranny they could possibly find. Unfortunately thirty minutes later they were still stumped. They reconvened in the living room, having checked everything but the kitchen.

"I wish we had an idea what we were looking for," Nelson said.

"I know," Kanen replied. "Anything from paperwork to computer disks or USB keys. It could even be a photograph. We won't know the significance until we find it."

Taking sections of the kitchen, they carefully pulled out

every drawer and checked through them, even under them. When he'd gone through the cutlery drawer, Kanen put the drawer back in and pushed to close it, but something caught. He crouched so he could see better and found an envelope taped to the underside.

He made a light crowing sound. The others gathered around. He untaped it and held it in his hand. "Just a blank envelope on the outside," he murmured, "taped but not sealed." He opened it up. Inside he pulled out money, three bills. In between a couple of them was a photograph of someone standing in front of a building. Kanen stared at it, then held it up for the other two to see.

"Do you recognize that face?" Nelson asked.

"It's Blake," Kanen said quietly. "But I have no clue what this means." He turned the photo over. The date on the back was two days before Blake died. Kanen frowned. "Now that is ominous. Blake died two days after this photo was taken." Kanen checked the money and realized the bills were sequential. He walked over to the kitchen table, laid them down in the order they were numbered. Behind each printed serial number were two neatly printed handwritten numbers. He grabbed a pen and a notepad from his pocket and wrote those down. A total of six digits: 263947. He looked at the numbers and then to the men. "Any ideas?"

They shook their heads, frowning.

After a moment, Nelson offered a few guesses. "Safe-deposit box number? Bank account number?"

Taylor added, "It's got to be something."

Kanen pulled out his phone and dialed Laysa. When she answered, he said, "Listen to this number," and he rattled it off. "Mean anything to you?"

Her voice was hesitant when she answered. "It doesn't

sound like a bank account of ours. I'm not sure. Why?"

"Because we found an envelope under your cutlery drawer with three one-dollar bills in sequence. After each of the serial numbers is a pair of handwritten numbers, and that's what these six numbers are." Then the air caught in his throat. "I wonder if they should be read as 26-39-47." He caught the knowing looks in the other men's gazes.

"I don't understand what difference that makes," she said.

"Do you have a locked safe somewhere? This could be a combination number."

"I don't know," she said. "I don't think we ever had a safe where we lived. So I can't imagine what that combination would be for."

"Did he have a locker somewhere, like maybe for a gym membership?"

"Sure, he has a gym membership—well, *had* a gym membership," she corrected. "And he kept a locker there."

"Any idea if the locker is still in his name?"

"I'm not sure," she said slowly. "I never paid any more gym bills. But I think it was paid for annually. I just don't know when that twelve-month period started."

"What gym was it?"

"Gold's Training Center," she said. "He was good friends with Mark, the manager."

"Okay, we'll call you back." Kanen hung up, turned to the guys and said, "Blake was a member of Gold's Training Center. Kept a locker there."

The men pulled up the address. "It's open now," Taylor said. "Why don't we take a quick look?"

"Done."

Kanen turned to look around the kitchen. "Everybody

checked everything possible? We don't want to assume this is the only thing here."

"That should be everything," Nelson said. "She doesn't have an attic here. The ceiling is at a uniform height throughout her apartment and made of wood—not some drop-down temporary panels to hide ductwork or whatever. And there is no optional storage to rent elsewhere in the apartment building. The only thing we haven't done is pull out the fridge and the stove."

The men looked at each other, and Kanen nodded. "Let's do that first."

It didn't take much effort, but they found nothing more. With all the appliances back in place, they took one last look around.

Kanen nodded to the front door. "Let's check out Gold's."

It took ten minutes before they were parked in front of the gym. "This is the building Blake is standing in front of in the picture found with the money. I remember that door trim." They walked in side by side.

One of the staff looked up, smiled at them and said, "What can we do for you?"

"Did you know Blake Elliott?"

The man's face twisted with sadness. "Yeah, I did. He was a good mate."

"Does he still have a locker here?"

"Who's asking?"

Kanen identified himself and then said, "I can get Laysa Elliot to call you, if you want."

Instead the man—whose shirt identified him as Mark, the manager—picked up the phone and dialed a number. "Laysa, I have three men here, asking permission to see inside Blake's locker. You okay with that?"

The two discussed the problem as Kanen watched.

When Mark hung up, he said, "Okay, she's good with it. Honestly, his year's membership would be up in another week or so. I would have called Laysa about it anyway. Should have done it earlier. I guess I just figured I'd give her some time. Come on. It's this way." He led them through the equipment room into the back.

In the changing rooms were banks of lockers, some half size, some quarter size, some full size. He tapped Blake's full-size locker at one end of a bank of lockers and said, "This is it. But I'm not sure I like breaking into it."

Kanen stepped forward and said, "I might have the combination."

He tried the first sequence of numbers. When that didn't work, he did them in reverse. As soon as the third number was dialed, the tumblers fell into place, and the lock clicked apart.

Mark stepped back and said, "Well, that's a relief. It feels like a violation as it is. But I'd hate to cut off that lock."

Realizing Mark spoke as a friend and somebody who had also lost someone close to him, Kanen nodded in understanding. "I hear you. Blake was too good a man to die so young."

Kanen studied the contents of the locker: a jacket, a pair of running pants, a pair of shoes, a pair of socks. He saw a bag with something in it sitting on the floor of the locker. On the shelf above, he couldn't quite see what was there, but it looked like a book bag. He picked up the jacket, handed it to Taylor to check, the pants went to Nelson, and Kanen grabbed the sneakers and the socks.

Finally Mark asked, "What are you looking for?"

"Anything. Nothing in particular," Kanen said absent-mindedly. He turned and looked at Mark. "Do you have a plastic bag, so we can return Blake's belongings to Laysa?"

Mark nodded and took off.

The three looked at each other, and Taylor said, "The jacket is clean. So are the pants. So are the shoes and the socks apparently."

With everything folded and stacked to the side, Kanen pulled out the bag on the bottom, and they opened it up to see a water bottle, a fitness watch—one of the latest and best of course—plus a journal where Blake kept track of his progress and his weights. That was it in there.

Kanen reached for the bag on the top shelf. What had looked like a book bag was a leather travel bag. He crouched down with it in front of them and opened the zipper. Inside unsealed envelopes with photos spilling out. He pulled out one envelope and flipped through the photos, then stopped to study a picture of one man who was vaguely familiar. He held it up to the others to take a look. "Anyone know who this is?"

"No, but these look like blackmail photos," Nelson said immediately.

The men exchanged grim looks. Kanen put the photos back into the bag, zipped it up, handed it to Nelson for safekeeping and went through the rest of the locker one more time. When it was confirmed as fully emptied, Mark returned with a plastic bag. They packed it up with Blake's belongings.

Kanen shook Mark's hand and said, "Thanks. We appreciate this." He turned, and the group walked back outside.

"Where to now?" Nelson asked.

"We need to go through this blackmail collection very closely," Taylor said. "Maybe take backup photos, so nothing's lost."

Kanen nodded. "I agree. But where?"

"Our hotel would be best," Taylor suggested. "If we go to her apartment, we might find *him* there as well."

Kanen pulled out his phone and called Laysa. When she answered, her voice was sleepy. "Did I wake you up?"

"No, I'm just dozing," she said softly. "All of this is bringing up memories."

"I'm so sorry," he said.

"No, you don't understand. They are good memories. I miss Blake a lot, but we had a good life, and I realized I'm starting to deal with the loss instead of denying it."

"That's progress then," he said, "but it's still difficult to finally accept the loss. It's a process. Give yourself time. So far, we have not yet gone through the storage unit. But we did find something, and we need to figure it out."

"What did you find?" Her voice was sharp.

"We don't know yet. I didn't want to open anything there in the gym, with all those prying eyes."

"So where can I meet you? Because I want to see this too."

"*Hmm*," he said, frowning.

"Don't try to stop me," she snapped. "This is about Blake's life and about finding that asshole who invaded my home, who held me captive."

"I hear you," he said quietly. "But it might not be that easy a chore."

"Neither was getting beaten up by that asshole, all for whatever you found. If not my place, another place or your hotel. Just name it. I'll be there."

"We'll meet in the lobby of my hotel," he said. "Make that fifteen minutes from now?"

"I'm already leaving a note and walking out of Carl's apartment," she snapped. "I should be there in ten. Make sure you guys are there."

He grinned, hung up and told the others what was going on. "Let's go. She doesn't wait well for anybody."

"She's definitely a woman with a mind of her own."

"That she is."

"Did they have a good relationship?" Taylor's voice was bland, but his gaze was intent as he studied Kanen's face.

Kanen nodded. "They'd been in love since forever. They were best friends who fell in love with each other."

"Were you and her ever together?" Nelson asked.

Kanen laughed. "No. The first time she saw Blake, that was all there was room for in her life. I never quite made the cut."

"That's okay too," Nelson said. "If you wanted a chance, now is a good time."

"Oh, no you don't," Kanen said, shaking his head at them. "Nothing like that is going on between the two of us."

"I don't know about that," Taylor said. "I saw how she was in your arms this morning."

"Absolutely," Kanen said. "But that's what friends are for. To comfort each other. So ... *no matchmaking.*"

"No matches have to be made," Nelson said with a big grin. "Looks like the match has already *been* made."

Kanen hopped into their rental car and turned on the engine. "That's so wrong," he muttered.

"No, it so isn't wrong. She can hold her own. She'd be prime girlfriend material for a SEAL. We're delighted for you," Taylor said, humor in his tone.

"Don't be," Kanen replied. "That would be like stepping on toes or betraying my best friend. That's something I can't ever do."

"But it's not," Nelson argued. "Look at it from the other side. Blake's not here to be with her, to look after her. He'd be happy to know she was safe and sound with you. He doesn't want her to be alone for the rest of her life. If the two of you are together, you know he'll be up there, smiling down on you and saying, 'Dude, go for it, with my blessing.'"

The trouble was, the way Nelson had said that sounded just like Blake. An eerie voice out of Kanen's past looking down on him. It gave Kanen a hell of a shock. It also made him think. Was that what Blake would be happy with? Kanen and Blake had been best buds. That had never been a question before. But what about now? Would Blake be happy, and would he say something like that? As Kanen thought about it, he realized Blake, being who Blake was, would say *exactly* that.

CHAPTER 5

S HE SAT IN the lobby five minutes ahead of their appointed time; she couldn't wait much longer. She didn't understand what Kanen and his men had found, but obviously the trip to the gym had been worthwhile. It was early in the day. She kept watch on the front entrance, even as the hotel manager kept watch on her.

With relief she saw the men move through the lobby with the same surety her husband had had.

Like somebody in command of his life. A man in charge of his destiny. She'd always admired that sense of confidence in Blake.

She'd never had it herself and recognized how valuable it was in others. Blake had always just laughed it off as being nothing. But it wasn't *nothing*. He was somebody who had lived life to the fullest and who understood what he could handle and what he couldn't. She'd always felt like she handled life well, but then everybody around her protected her and stopped her from fully experiencing hardships. And maybe that was a good thing. She tended to be an all-or-nothing kind of person. Like meeting Blake. When she did, she'd fallen instantly. Yes, they were best friends first, but she knew. Probably long before Blake did. There'd never been anyone else for her.

Thankfully he'd felt the same all along their relationship

trail—as they shifted from best friends to lovers, then got married. When she lost him, her world had fallen apart. He'd been everything to her—in a very real and tangible way. For the longest time she didn't want to live, had nobody—outside of Kanen—who really cared if she lived or died, other than maybe her students. She had curled up in a cold ball of pain and had refused to acknowledge the world around her. But she had a job to keep and kids to teach, and she now needed that job in order to pay her bills, so she was forced to get up and go to school every day. And that was all fine and dandy until coming home at the end of the day ... alone. Reminded of her loss each night.

Kanen had been a huge part of her life. A good friend long before she and Blake were married, Kanen had been a much closer friend since she lost Blake. And she knew perfectly well her friendship with Kanen would be there forever. They'd been through a lot together. When she had miscarried, she had cried to Kanen. Blake had understood, but he was more philosophical about it, ... maybe even relieved.

He'd said it hadn't seemed real to him yet, not a child he could see and hold. But Kanen had seemed to understand. That had endeared him to her like nothing else. She and Blake had kept trying, but conception never happened again. When she lost Blake, how she wished to have had his child, a piece of him, someone to hug, to love, to care for. Instead she just had memories from a lot of years together. Kanen had made a point of reminding her how she'd lived life to the fullest with Blake during their best-friends period into their dating period and then their marriage. That she should rejoice in having had the opportunity to have shared all those years with Blake.

Cerebrally she knew Kanen was right. In her heart though, it didn't matter—she wanted it all. She wanted another fifty years with Blake, sitting side by side in their rocking chairs on a porch, holding hands—although Blake had often said that he wouldn't live that long.

He was a bit of a risk-taker, a hell-bent-for-leather kind of guy. But that in itself was okay too. She'd been the opposite. She'd always erred on the safe side. Maybe that was what had attracted her to him. He was the opposite of safe. When he went snowboarding, he was forever going out of bounds and taking risks. When he had his Harley— thankfully, she had talked him into selling that motorcycle soon after they married—it was the same thing, always going way too fast, never really caring if he lived or died, because he lived full-out in every moment. Whereas she sat at home, waiting, hoping he would return to her safe and whole. She never understood that adrenaline-junkie side to him. But it hadn't mattered because she'd loved it anyway. She had loved it because she had loved him.

That didn't mean she liked it. She didn't like the fact that, when he said he'd be home, he didn't come home for a couple hours afterward, and she'd worry and fret before he'd walk in with a silly grin on his face, wrap her up tight in a hug and cuddle her close, and all her worries would go away.

As she brooded on her memories, the men stepped in front of her. Kanen reached down a hand, and she let him help her to her feet. "Don't you look pleased with yourself."

His grin slipped. "Let's go up to the room."

She followed the men to the elevator. They didn't say a word but neither did Kanen let go of her hand. It was hard to know what to think, but she trusted him. And, if he thought this was the best thing to do, then that was fine with her.

At their suite, she walked straight in to find they had a huge suite, with a couch in the central living room area and two large bedrooms with two big beds in each off on opposite sides. She sat down at the far corner of the couch. "So will you talk now?"

Kanen dropped a leather bag on the coffee table. "Do you recognize this bag?"

She looked at it and frowned. "No, I don't think I've seen it before."

He sat beside her on the couch and unzipped the bag.

She leaned forward to see envelopes with photos of all different sizes inside. "What's all this?"

"What we found in Blake's locker at the gym."

"Really? I don't remember ever seeing this."

Kanen nodded. "That's why I'm asking if you know the bag."

Her gaze zipped back to the bag itself. She couldn't remember ever seeing something like this. As a rule Blake liked modern contemporary, manly looking stuff. And this was definitely masculine, but it was older looking. Oval with odd straps, it reminded her of a man's manicure kit but on a much larger scale.

"It's not something he would normally go for," she said slowly. "He had a matching set of luggage, and everything he had was pretty perfect, if you remember," she said, sliding a look toward Kanen.

"I was thinking that myself," he said. "I'm not sure if this is what your captor was looking for or if it's something else entirely." He pulled out an envelope and very carefully upended all the photos onto the coffee table.

She studied them, her mind not really comprehending.

"Lots of these are of the same people," she noted, reaching forward to group related photos together. Her face scrunched up when she saw several were of people having sex. "Good Lord, where did Blake get these, and why would anybody want them?" She shuffled through the very flagrant ones, quickly setting them aside. As she continued to sort the photos, she said, "Not only have I never seen these photos but I don't know any of the people in them."

Unlike her, the men sat on the floor on the opposite side of the coffee table and carefully went through every photo, as if studying the facial features of each person. She watched their actions and knew they didn't care about what activities the couples were involved in. The men were just trying to identify who was in the photos.

"Do you know any of them?" she asked them. At their headshakes, she glanced at Kanen. "Do *you* know any of them?"

"No, I don't recognize any of these men."

Sectioning off another portion of the coffee table, he opened up a second envelope and carefully laid out those photos. This time, instead of dumping them, he pulled them out one by one and put them on the table.

Once done, Kanen took the leather bag to the table and proceeded to empty all the other envelopes. He laid the contents on the empty surface, so they were all spread out, and so everybody could take a look. Trying to be as methodical as possible, Laysa systematically went through every one of the photos, wincing at some of the compromising positions. There were photos not only of men with women but also of men with men and some of women with women.

She personally was of the opinion that everybody should have the right to be happy, and, as long as they weren't hurting anyone else, their sexual preferences were their own. But what if these were prominent figures—and ones who hadn't gone public about their lifestyle? Or what if they were married and their spouses had no idea?

As she stared at the one in her hand, she realized what this was all about. "These are blackmail photos, aren't they?"

Kanen walked toward her. He took a look at the photo in her hand and shrugged. "It's quite likely they all are, yes."

"You can't think Blake had something to do with this, do you?" She hated the worried note that entered her voice because no way she would believe Blake was involved in any of this nastiness. Surely his best friend wouldn't believe it of him either. Warmth filled her heart as Kanen shook his head.

"I know Blake as well as you do," he said softly. "This isn't his style. However, it does make sense that maybe this is the material he was asked to keep."

"Do you think Blake knew what was in the bag?" She waved an arm over the photos. "Do you think he knew what he was asked to keep?" She couldn't stop worrying about the fact that maybe Blake had compromised his own sense of honor by allowing this to come into his possession.

"I guess I would have a hard time," Taylor said, "if somebody I respected asked me to keep a bag for them. I'd want to know what was in it. And, once left in my possession, I would probably open it," he admitted. "Because, as a general rule of thumb, someone you respect shouldn't ask this of you."

She winced at that thought because she figured she would want to know too. "Blake might have asked," she said cautiously. "He might have accepted the man's version of what was in here."

"How do the dollar bills and the combination numbers

fit in with this from Blake's point of view?" Nelson wondered out loud.

"Blake was a lover of all things puzzles," Laysa said. "He loved to hide things—my anniversary present, birthday gift, an extra Christmas surprise—then give me clues to find them."

"He certainly did like to make things convoluted," Kanen agreed. "He used to write down clues for where to meet him later in the day, like is done for scavenger hunts, leading us on a merry chase."

"Maybe Blake was following instructions himself. Maybe he felt he needed to be cautious—maybe thinking his friend was in trouble?" Nelson theorized.

Kanen stared off in the distance.

She studied Kanen's face, worried that all of this would change his impression of his best friend. Impulsively she said, "I don't think Blake had anything to do with it."

Surprised, Kanen turned to look at her, saying, "I don't think he had anything to do with the blackmail, no. Was this just some joke, some game? I don't know. I mean, if you consider how Blake and I talked all the time, who else did he talk to? Can you think of anyone who'd know him this well?"

She shook her head. "No one. And I certainly didn't recognize my captor's physique or voice."

"But Blake had to have another best buddy, another best friend," Taylor said. "No way he couldn't have bonded in the navy, with the teams and the closeness of the units. Once he left the navy, especially moving to England, it must have deprived him of many of those friends. He had to make new ones. Because you don't store something like this for somebody who wasn't a friend. If Kanen had called Blake and had asked him to do something like this, Blake would have done it in a heartbeat. And vice versa."

"But, if he'd been in any kind of trouble, he would have told me before it came to this," Kanen said. "And that's the interesting point here. Because we were such good friends, Blake would have come to me if there was a problem."

"So, from that, we can gather this wasn't a problem for Blake," Nelson said. "And the guy who owned these wasn't as good a friend as you were."

"So we're looking for somebody who was a good friend but not a best friend," Taylor said. He twisted to look at Laysa. "What about at Blake's work? Was he close to somebody there?"

She sank into the corner of the couch, a little more unnerved at the thought of somebody in Blake's life who she didn't know about. Of course he had had friends, but she thought she knew everyone in his immediate circle. "He didn't talk about work much. At the time I never really worried about it. After he left the navy, he wanted to leave the States and for some reason chose to go into sales in the medical equipment field. Strictly in-house, no traveling. Surprised me that he wanted office work. I know he was constantly busy with stacks of files and always trying to drum up more sales. Like some telemarketer salesman.

"I didn't understand that choice, but I wanted Blake to be happy and to spend my life with him. So, of course, we came here. But I don't remember him ever talking about anybody more than once. A couple people in the office he didn't like. A couple people in the office he thought were useless. A couple people had come and gone over the years who he had no appreciation for. One guy he really did like, but he moved away about two years ago."

"Do you remember what his name was?"

She looked up at Kanen and shook her head. "No, I don't. I'm not sure I ever knew it. Blake just came home one day pretty upset because the only decent person in the office had just quit. He did go out and meet him for a beer a couple weeks later. As far as I know, the guy left the country." She tried to recall the memories from way back when. "It was actually three years ago now, but maybe he returned to the US." Laysa sagged in place as she contemplated what that could mean. "But it's not as if we can say he's the guy who invaded my home and beat me up."

"If he went back to the US, then what would bring him back here again?" Taylor asked.

"No idea," Laysa said. "My captor said *the situation had changed,* and he needed his insurance policy back." She stared at the blackmail photos. "Is that what these are—his insurance?"

"It would make sense," Kanen said. "But why now? Either he stopped blackmailing people and will start again or he knows someone is using these photos as blackmail and plans to do something about it."

"And that will get even more confusing," Taylor said, rubbing a hand to his forehead. "That last suggestion does make a kind of sense. But then you're looking at this asshole as an almost good guy."

"That is what's wrong with this," she said. "These are actual photos. He should still have the digital files."

KANEN LOOKED AT her in surprise. "You're right. If he gave these to Blake even a couple years ago, we had digital cameras back then—our phones took better photos than these—which means, chances are, these are quite old photos." He looked at them to study the backs of several photos and said, "No dates are on them. That's another odd thing. What kind of camera takes pictures without dating them?"

"A lot of the older ones did," Taylor said. "We could assume these are old enough that they came from film that had been developed. There are still a few cameras like that around but not many. But what are the chances that this guy hasn't digitized these photos? It would be easy enough to scan them in, so why wouldn't he have already done that?"

"He *would* have done that," she said in surprise. "No way this is the only copy you have and that you'd leave them with somebody and take off for other parts of the world without having a backup, would you?"

Kanen chuckled softly and sat beside her, patting her knee. "That's the way to think. You and I certainly wouldn't have done that, so I highly doubt your captor did either."

"So then why does he care about these photos?"

The others looked at each other for a long moment.

Then Nelson offered slowly, "Maybe he's lost the digital copy."

"That can happen," Taylor said. "We've all lost digital files. Supposed to be nothing safer but computer files get corrupt, files get lost, the hard drive fails, electronics get junked that shouldn't have been, and you can never find the files again. Obviously, he should have taken very good care of whatever he had in a digital file, but maybe he wasn't doing cloud storage back then. Maybe it was on a hard drive, and he thought it was safe, and then he dropped the hard drive, or it was corrupted in another way. Maybe he lost the thumb drive backup. It could be any of these reasons."

The others nodded, deep in thought.

"That would imply," Laysa said, "that he needs the insurance so he can get a digital copy again, and this is the only copy he has in order to either keep the blackmail rolling or to stop something or someone else."

Kanen sat back. "So what's our responsibility here? This guy wants his photos back. At least, let's consider these are his for the moment. Is there any reason we can't give them to him?"

"Yes," she said, her voice strong, hard. "If these people in the photos don't know he has these, no way I'm giving them back to him."

Nelson grinned at her. "It's nice to know you're honorable. But do you realize that you're pitting your life against these photos?"

Her stomach twisted with nausea. "Surely there's another way than that."

"Nelson is certainly stating the situation in a blunt way," Kanen said. "He is just trying to make you understand how serious this could get."

"There's another option," Taylor said. "We could scan these ourselves. It wouldn't take long. At least then we could potentially contact these people to let them know what the photos are about and where they were taken." At her frowning stare, Taylor answered what was probably her next question. "We'd use facial-recognition software to ID the people if possible. Then we'd use geodata to confirm the location."

"Okay, and then what?" she asked. "If we can't stop the blackmailer, having duplicates just doubles our problem. We could have the asshole after us and also the people in all these photos."

Kanen interrupted. "Our theories are taking us down a very narrow path of possibilities. There could be other options, even if I can't think of what they are at the moment."

She frowned at him.

He laced her fingers with his. "All I'm saying is, keep an open mind."

She pointed at the mostly nude couple in bed. "If that was me, I would want to know every copy of every photo was in my hands."

"That's the problem with the internet," Taylor said. "You can't guarantee that anymore. The internet sends out digital copies forever. It would be almost impossible to destroy these permanently."

She nodded. "Which is the problem with us scanning them in to share with … one of your guys, I guess. Because then we're duplicating the process, right?"

Kanen sat back and studied her face. "Do you have another suggestion?"

She shook her head. "No, not at the moment, but I wish I knew who these people were, so I could return the photos to them."

"Or we could burn them," Nelson suggested. "Then they don't belong to anybody."

"But what if these people *are* being blackmailed?" she asked. "What if they are being blackmailed and are paying for these photos and never get a copy? Maybe they've been shown digital copies, but these are the originals." She tapped several of the photos on the coffee table. "Which kind of makes sense. These people being blackmailed might want the originals, even knowing the blackmailer could have digital copies still, and then it's up to them to decide if it's worth continuing to pay the blackmail."

"Well, obviously the blackmailer didn't send the damning photos via email," Taylor mentioned. "Otherwise the blackmailer could get a copy of those photos from his Sent folder."

She nodded. "Yes, the attachments are always there. Unless he's locked out of his account."

"It's more likely that he dropped off an envelope with a copy of the picture and his demands. Keeping it anonymous," Kanen said. "The thing is, we have to find out if these *are* blackmail photos. Is your captor a blackmailer? Or does he need these pictures for another purpose, like to save his own hide?"

At that, he felt Laysa start. She turned, staring into his face, and asked, "Is that even a possibility?"

"He invaded your home. He held you against your will there," Kanen said. "He beat you up in order to get information from you. But, if he was really dangerous, he could have killed you or shot you in the leg or wherever."

"He threatened to kill me. But would he have done that before getting his insurance policy?" she asked, looking at the men, who largely remained silent. That made her worry even more. "Plus ... he wanted *you* here, Kanen, so he could get this information. Maybe it's more about Kanen and less about the photos. The fact is, I'm half expecting my attacker to walk through that damn door any moment. Something was really, really creepy about him."

"He did break into your apartment, beat you and hold you captive. So he'll seem creepy and scary and pretty damn evil in your mind for a while. To me, he's just another piece of shit, trying to bend another person to his will. Whether he's trying to save his own skin or trying to blackmail these people, it doesn't matter to me. I'm going after him for what he did to you."

He watched tears come to her eyes, and she smiled mistily up at him. He shook his head and wrapped his arms around her. "How can you think I wouldn't be here to help you? Of course I'm pissed off at what he's done. That's not acceptable. But to batter and bruise somebody I know and care about, well, that'll never go down well."

"If you two are done reminiscing about how much you care about each other," Nelson teased, "potentially you could turn all that energy into figuring out how we'll deal with this from here on in."

"I still think we should scan these to use facial recognition software, so we can identify them," Taylor stated. "Then we can contact these people and find out if they *are* being blackmailed. It's possible these photos are being held for a future time. If any of them are political figures, then there might be better times in their careers to be blackmailed, to get something from them or to ruin their careers. Think about elections coming up or bills being passed. If you wanted to sway the political leanings of somebody, nothing like having some nice little photos in your possession to make them do what you want."

She shuddered. "That's terrible."

The men just laughed.

"We deal with this on a global level," Taylor said. "But it all comes down to one man who's usually leading the pack, pushing from behind to get his wants met."

Kanen had seen way too many democracies fall under the power of one man in third-world countries. It was usually about power. It was rarely about the people. He tapped the photos. "Okay, we'll scan these. We'll keep them in a zip file. Who can do the facial recognition?"

"MI6 or maybe Tesla," Taylor said. "She is about the only one with that kind of software which we can access and keep it private. That's if she's available. These people might be too old now for that application anyway. I don't know."

Kanen nodded. He pulled out his phone and sent Mason a text, then glanced at Laysa. "Do you have a scanner at your house?"

She nodded. But she didn't look happy about it.

"May we use it, if we promise this material will never fall into the wrong hands?" It still didn't make her look much happier.

"You can't promise that though, can you? Already you're talking about sending it to someone, which means it'll always be available on the internet."

She was right, and nothing he could do would make her feel any better about that truth. But still, it was what needed to happen.

CHAPTER 6

S HE DIDN'T LIKE Kanen's plan, but it was the only one they had. They crossed the lobby of the hotel only to be suddenly surrounded by several official-looking men in suits.

"It's barely eight in the morning. It's too early for this," Kanen grumbled to the guys.

Laysa came to a confused stop, looked up and said, "Gentlemen, may I help you?"

The three men she was with stepped up beside her, forcing the others to step back.

One of the strangers stepped forward, the other two behind him now, as he held up a hand and said, "We need to talk."

Kanen stepped in front of Laysa. "Identification please," he said, his tone hard.

The two suited men exchanged assessing gazes before the stranger in charge carefully pulled an ID card out of his upper chest pocket. He held it out for Kanen to look at. Of course nobody offered it to her. Kanen studied it, and she caught just the barest grimace cross his face.

She turned to look at the man and said, "I presume you're some special government officer?"

The man chuckled. "We're MI6," he said in a lazy voice. "Julian Normandy, at your service. I understand you might be involved in something a little nasty."

She nodded. "Maybe you can help."

"We're hoping we can." He turned and motioned toward a big black vehicle, like a cross between a sedan and an SUV, sitting outside the hotel's front door. "We'll ask you to join us for a talk."

She headed forward without hesitation. But obviously the three men with her weren't too happy. She glanced at Kanen. "Is this a bad idea?"

He sighed. "No, but it's a curtailing of freedom." He motioned at the man whose ID he'd been given. "Julian has been sent to keep an eye on us while we're here."

"Both informally and formally, depending if you're here officially or unofficially," Julian said with a grin.

She was ushered into the middle seat in the sedan with Kanen on one side and Nelson on the other. It was almost a limo with three rows of front-facing seats. Taylor was in the last bench seat behind her with the two men who had been with Julian. MI6 had a driver waiting in the car, and Julian climbed in to take the front passenger seat. By the time they were all packed inside, and the vehicle was on the move, she turned to Julian and asked, "How did you know we were in trouble?"

"Charles, in a roundabout way."

She frowned. "I don't know Charles," she said hesitantly.

"I do," Kanen said. "But I didn't expect him to call in the reinforcements."

"No, but I think he found something he thought made the two of us meeting up a good idea."

That was unnerving. She stared out the window. "Are we going to Charles's place then?" she asked hopefully. "We really have a situation we don't know how to handle."

Kanen stiffened at her side, but she ignored him. She didn't live in his world of ugliness, and she knew her husband hadn't either. Whatever was going on now was foreign to her, and that made it a very uncomfortable and uneasy place to be. Any help would be appreciated.

"Would you care to explain?" Julian asked.

"My husband died just under a year ago," she said slowly. "Apparently sometime before he died, he was asked to hold something by a man he knew. And he did so without letting me know. Now this person has come back looking for it. He broke into my apartment and held me captive while he searched. He couldn't find it, so he slapped me around to try to get information as to where it was."

At that, Julian crossed his arms and glared at her. "And you didn't call the police?"

She didn't like his tone. She stiffened her back and gave him a hard look. "I was a captive at the time, so I could hardly do it then, could I?"

"But you did get free. Why didn't you call for assistance then?"

She widened her eyes in a look she had perfected a long time ago and said gently, "I did. I contacted Carl, who is in law enforcement. Not to mention at the hospital, the local forensic techs collected DNA and took photos. My assailant had forced me to contact Kanen. So, of course, I had to contact him again when I got free. He's a good friend, so I turned to him for help."

Julian looked at her in surprise, turned to look at Kanen and then back at her. "You're living in England. You have law enforcement all around you. You have *government* law enforcement all around you. And yet, you call an American to come over here and help you? You didn't want to wait for this Carl person to get in touch with the right people?"

"Kanen was already on the way after the first call from my captor. Of course, when Kanen arrived, I followed his lead. It's what he does. He's also a friend, so that was the best thing for me to do."

Julian stared at her in disbelief. "That's not a normal thing to do."

She crossed her arms over her chest, almost imitating him, and leaned back. "I trust Kanen. He was my husband's best friend too. He's also a navy SEAL, although that's not for public knowledge. He and his buddies handle this kind of stuff all the time. If there was anybody I could count on to help me, it was him. My captor insisted I call Kanen because the asshole figured, if I wasn't holding the material, then Kanen would be."

"That makes more sense. Did you ever meet this guy?" Julian turned to ask Kanen.

Kanen shook his head and picked up the story. "Her attacker wore a mask, so we have no facial features to go by. Laysa didn't recognize his voice but noted he was short for a man, and yet, very muscular with extremely wide feet. So, no, I don't believe I've ever met this guy. But we haven't found him, so I can't confirm that yet. And you can bet that, when I do, he won't be talking much."

JULIAN'S FROWN DEEPENED.

Kanen shook his head. "Don't give me that look. This guy holds a single woman hostage in her apartment and beats her up for information she doesn't have. Surely you expect me to at least break the bully's jaw."

Julian appeared to think it wasn't worth arguing about.

"Did you find out what it was he was looking for?"

"Possibly," Laysa said cautiously.

"And that's where I'm supposed to help?" Julian asked, raising one eyebrow.

"No, the only help we need is a ride back to her apartment," Kanen snapped.

Julian glared at him.

Just then Kanen's phone rang. He put it to his ear. "Mason, I'm in an MI6 vehicle, taken to an undetermined location. If you don't hear from us in the next twenty-four hours, you know we've been sunk deep in the ocean."

Mason's lazy voice rolled through the phone and into the vehicle. "I presume that will not happen. Julian, is that you?"

Kanen hit the Speaker button so everybody in the vehicle could hear.

"Hello, Mason. You could have told me yourself what was going on."

"I would have if they had brought me up to date on any of it," Mason said. "But it seems to have all just happened, so I couldn't update you, could I? But I presume Charles has been kept in the loop somehow."

"Yes," Kanen said. "I gave him updates as we were moving about Ipswich, just in case something went south."

Laysa stared at him in surprise. "I think I'd like to meet this Charles."

Kanen laced his fingers with hers. "He's a very honorable ex-military benefactor. He's helped a lot of men."

Julian laughed.

"That's not a bad way to describe him. And he is, indeed, the one who called me," Mason said. "Did you send him a photo?"

"Yes," Kanen said. "I took a picture of one of the photos we found and sent it to Charles, hoping he could ID the man."

Julian nodded. "That's the one he sent to me. So now we're all together on the same page." His smile was big and bright with a tinge of hardness to it.

She didn't need this jockeying around for position. "I get all of this who's-in-charge stuff is important to you guys, but what's important to me is that we catch this asshole. I don't know why he wants this stuff. I don't know what he'll do with it. I don't know who he is or where he came from. I don't want these photos floating around for anyone to see. And I *really* don't want him coming back after me." She leaned forward and glared at Julian. "Got it?"

Surprised at her tonal aberration, Julian smiled at her. "Got it."

Mason chuckled. "Nice to meet you, Laysa. I'm one of Kanen's team members."

Beside her, Kanen leaned over and said, "Essentially he's the boss but with lots of bigger bosses above him."

She nodded. She had asked Kanen years ago for an explanation of how all that military stuff had worked, and he'd given her a brief outline, but it hadn't made a whole lot of sense. An awful lot of titles were involved. She wasn't sure who did all the work. "So then why are you taking us anywhere?" Laysa asked Julian.

"We need a place to talk obviously," Julian said, "and inside this vehicle is private."

She glanced at Kanen.

He shook his head. "No, it's not. It'll be bugged."

Julian looked at him in surprise. "No, it won't be."

Taylor snorted. "Shall I run a test then?"

Julian looked at him. "If you have something on you, go ahead."

Taylor was in the seat behind her. She couldn't see what he was doing. She heard a weird hum behind her as he turned in the vehicle and slowly shifted around, as if searching for something.

When he was finally done, he sat back and said, "It's clean."

Julian looked at him. "How could you suspect anything less?"

"Are *you* recording this conversation?" Kanen asked.

"Should we be?"

"You didn't answer my question."

"*We* should then," Taylor stated.

"Stop," Laysa snapped. "Keep all your posturing to yourselves. This is not about who has rights, who has ownership of this problem. We're Americans. And we're on British soil. And these navy men are here to help protect me as much as anything."

"That's the theory," Taylor said.

"Yes, that is the theory," Julian said helpfully. "But the photo that Charles sent us is of one of our current ambassadors. A man of some prominence. And those photos are not ones we've ever seen before. They aren't for public consumption, and that means somebody's violated his privacy, and there has to be a reason why."

"The only reason we can think of," she said, "well, based on my assailant's comment to me about wanting his *insurance policy* back, as things have changed, ... is likely blackmail. Maybe he lost his digital copies and now needs the physical images."

Julian blinked at her a couple times, processing her convoluted explanation. Then he smiled. "That's all too possible. But these photos are quite old. So who is this attacker of yours, where did he get these photos, and what is he planning on doing with them if he gets them back now?"

"We were hoping you would answer that," she said. "My apartment building might have cameras. I don't know. If you could check who came and went, then maybe we'd find out who he is."

"The gym also has cameras," Kanen said. "I can check with the manager about security footage. That's where we found the bag with the photos. It's possible Laysa's assailant tried to get into Blake's gym locker too."

"But now you have the bag, these photos—correct?"

"We have something," Kanen said. "But I can't guarantee it's what the woman-beating asshole is looking for."

"Did you know about his gym locker?" Julian asked Laysa.

"I knew Blake went to the gym, and it was possible he had a locker there. I guess I just assumed he wouldn't keep anything valuable there."

"Did you need a key to get into it?"

"That's where things get a little odd," Kanen said. He explained about the money and the secret stash of currency that held the locker combination.

"That's very cloak-and-dagger stuff," Julian said. "Why would Blake do something so convoluted?"

Her laugh was strained to the point of almost hysteria. "Let's back up to a year ago and ask him," she snapped. "I have no clue. He was a huge movie buff with dinners afterwards to dissect what we watched. Maybe he saw somebody do something like that in a movie and thought it would work. Maybe he was afraid he'd forget the combination. Maybe this was how he managed to remind himself. I don't know why he did it. I didn't even know he had accepted this bag to begin with."

Kanen squeezed her fingers. "It'll be okay," he said quietly. "We're getting to the bottom of this. We will find this guy."

She closed her eyes and leaned back. "I hear what you're saying," she said. "I just wish we didn't have to dance around each other, so we could get on with it already."

Just then the vehicle pulled up outside her apartment building. She turned to Julian and asked, "Do you want to come up and take a look?"

He nodded. "Thank you. I would like that."

The vehicle parked, and all seven of them got out, the driver again remaining in the vehicle. She led the way to her apartment in silence. Everybody else followed her. At her door she stopped, her shoulders sagged. She looked over at Kanen. "I really don't want to do this."

He took the key from her and opened it.

Julian entered ahead of them.

Kanen said, "Remember that she was held here and beaten by that asshole. Show some sensitivity."

Julian nodded but didn't say a word.

Inside the apartment, nothing seemed to have changed. The MI6 men spread out and did a search. Julian came to the three of them standing in a half circle around Laysa and said, "Where did you find the money?"

Kanen led him to the kitchen drawer, pulled it back out and flipped it, so Julian could see where the tape had been. Then Kanen walked over to the coffee table, lifted a large Atlas and underneath it was the money as he had left it.

Still taped together, still in sequence.

"Interesting," Julian said. "Okay, so now let's get to the basics. Where are the photos?"

The men looked at each other, then turned and looked at Laysa.

She sighed. "You might as well show him. We would probably ask for their help anyway. We need to find out who all these people are."

Kanen took one of the envelopes of photos from an inside pocket to his jacket and lay them out on the kitchen table. The other two men with him did the same thing. By the time the entire kitchen table was full, they turned all the chairs sideways and filled them too.

Julian and his men stared.

"Wow," Julian said. "An awful lot of photos are here."

"Exactly. But we know none of the people in them," Kanen said. "This blackmailer appears to have a more European focus than American."

Julian tapped one of the photos and said, "This is a very prominent British family." He tapped another one. "This was a prominent British family who was accused of several major white-collar crimes and evaded being charged. They are now living in France."

They went through all the photos. Julian failed to recognize only six men.

"So we agree most of these men are in high positions of some kind, and whoever took these compromising photos thought they might be of monetary interest in some way to the people in these photos, correct?" Laysa asked.

The men all nodded.

"That would be a good guess," Julian said. "But these are old photos. Have these men been paying all this time? Did they pay, and this is just insurance that nobody says anything or insurance that the men are forever on the hook for?"

"That could also mean," one of Julian's men said, "what if one of these blackmailed men went after the blackmailer, found his stash and now this new blackmailer is looking to get even?"

"That's possible too," Julian said thoughtfully. "There're three or four likely scenarios. And I think we've touched on them all. None of the photos have dates on the backs."

"I wonder ..." Taylor said as he picked up a photo. "A smudge is on the back of each of them, as if some sort of acetate or vinegar solution might have erased the date stamp. Maybe a photo was taken, and it was recorded, but this way they're undated forever."

"And the advantage of that is what?" Laysa asked.

"Because they can be used over and over again."

Laysa's attention was caught by one photo. She stepped closer and squatted down beside the kitchen chair it was on. "She's very beautiful."

The men gathered around behind her.

One of Julian's men said, "I don't know the woman's name, but she married one of our members of parliament, Carlos ... somebody," he started. "Although I don't think he serves any longer. Didn't he retire to Spain?"

"He did," Julian confirmed.

Laysa said thoughtfully, "If he paid, this still could have had a great impact on his career. After all, the blackmailer could take the money and could then order Carlos to rule a certain way in parliament. The threat of the photo becoming public is a continuing one. ... What if Carlos wants to make sure this photo is gone forever?"

"It's possible. Any and all conjecture is possible," Kanen said. "But short of traveling to Spain and asking him and returning the photo, we won't know."

She shrugged. "I'd be happy to leave the country for a few days. Spain is only a quick hop away. Let's go."

Kanen turned to look at her.

"It's calling for rain in England anyway."

Kanen gave a boisterous laugh. "It's always calling for rain in England."

She beamed up at him. "So what better reason to go for a mini holiday then?"

Kanen chose to look at the MI6 men. "I presume none of you will speak to him?"

Julian grimaced. "No. And why would Carlos talk to you?"

"To tell him that his personal life is his own," Laysa replied, "and I thought maybe he would like this original photo."

"And then what? Just ask him if he was really having sex with her?" one of the MI6 men asked in a derisive tone.

Kanen stiffened and glared at him. "We're not confirming the veracity of the pictures. We're in search of an assailant who knows of the existence of these pictures and may have been the original blackmailer."

"Maybe Carlos can tell us something about him," she said thoughtfully. "Obviously you'll identify the six other men here who haven't already been ID'd, but then what? If you take away all these photos, I'll have a very angry captor returning, looking for goods he can't get back and that I can't give him."

Kanen pulled her toward him, wrapped his arms around her and tucked her close. "You don't have a lot of choice because MI6 is taking over this case."

Julian gave a bark of laughter. "We took it over the minute we heard about it. You guys were just slow to get the memo."

She turned to glare at him.

He held his hands up in mock surrender in front of him. "All in the best interests of keeping you safe, of course.

She rolled her eyes, making Kanen grin. "Then we'll be speaking to Carlos. Your agents can flutter around and look at these old photos. But I think the heart of the matter might be found in Spain."

"I'm willing and game if you are," Kanen said.

She smiled, took one look at Julian and asked, "Do you have any objection to us taking the five photos related to Carlos with us to Spain? I'd like to return those to him."

He shook his head. "Not at all. As long as we have a photo of the original pictures, I'm satisfied." He pointed at one of his men, who pulled out his phone and took a couple snapshots of each photo before handing over the five in question to Kanen. "But do keep in touch. There's no reason to think you'll be followed. But it's pretty easy for somebody to track you from one place to the next."

"We'll keep your advice in mind. But I have three knights of honor here, helping to keep me safe," she said with a big smile. "And we'll all enjoy a holiday in Spain."

Taylor chuckled as he stood at her side. "I've never been, so I'm in."

Nelson laughed. "I have been. But I'm all for going again."

"Decision made. We'll be in Spain." She took the pictures of the parliament member from Kanen. "Giving the originals back to Carlos."

"He may not want to talk to you," Julian warned. "This is a very sensitive issue."

"For that reason alone, he *will* talk to me," she said confidently. "If just to find out that it's over with."

CHAPTER 7

LAYSA WANTED TO dance. How long had she planned to
come to Spain? And here they were—10:50 a.m., two
and half hours after MI6 had dropped them at the airport
instead of their rental car at Kanen's hotel—the four of them
driving along the coast. Even though their reason for being
here was grim, it still felt in some ways like a holiday. A
holiday that she and Blake had wanted to take but just never
seemed to make happen. If ever a lesson was to be learned
about losing a loved one, it was to make the most of every
day.

It had taken her a long time to see the joy in any day
after losing him, but finally she had turned a corner. It was
good. Even in these circumstances, it was good.

Beside her Kanen asked, "What are you grinning about?"

"It feels good to be alive. And I owe you thanks for
that."

He raised an eyebrow. "I'm glad to hear you're feeling
better, but it's got nothing to do with me."

She reached for his hand. "Not true," she said. "Regardless of the reason, just having you back in my life, even
seeing you, has made me realize what a slump I had gotten
into and how I'd forgotten to see the joy in everything Blake
and I had. Do you realize we had always planned to come to
Spain for a holiday? And yet, somehow, even though we were

so close, we never did. That's just wrong."

"Quite true. It would have been a quick holiday for you. But we're here now, even though it's not a holiday and even though Blake isn't with us today," Kanen added. "I'm glad to hear you're happy about it regardless."

She smiled. "Very happy. Even more to realize I'm not caught in the depths of despair anymore," she said slowly. "I loved Blake with all my heart. Losing him was the most devastating event in my life. The suddenness of it. I guess there's no good way for somebody to die. I can't say I wanted him to suffer for five years just so I'd get five more years with him, but, when you wake up one day, and you don't know it'll be the last time you'll see somebody ... That was hard, and it reminded me just now how much we had planned to do that we never did. How much we wanted to do that we never made time for. I guess it's one of those lessons you never really understand until you go through something like this and realize how every day is precious."

There was silence in the vehicle as the men absorbed her revelation.

"I think, sadly, you're quite right about that," Nelson said. "Most of us don't learn these lessons the easy way. I think we get so caught up in everything we're doing that we forget to plan for things we might want to be doing."

"What does this trip to Spain mean to you?" Taylor asked Laysa. "I get that you're looking for answers about your own home invasion and assault, but is there anything else? A trip down memory lane for you and your husband perhaps?"

She was silent for a long moment while she thought about it. "I think it's just wanting to make the most of every day," she said quietly. "When we were married, we always thought there was time. We would do it next week, next month, next year, whatever. But it's amazing how much Blake's death and this home invasion event have cemented into my brain that I should take advantage of everything right now because there might not be another moment after this. I want answers to what this is all about, yes. Did we need to come to Spain? No, but it certainly wasn't a hardship. And, if I can make this man's life a little easier by handing back something he might be worried about, then I will do it."

"You realize he's likely to have the opposite reaction," Nelson said, waiting for her nod. "He might hold you responsible. He might think you're involved in some way. He could get ugly about this. He might be old enough that he's completely confused and has no clue what that photo is."

"I know," she said, pinching the bridge of her nose. "I realize my desire to do this is kind of an odd thought, and all those hypothetical responses from him are possible. Still, it got us out of England for a couple days while they track down my captor. I'm more than happy to wander Spain with you guys."

"Likewise," Taylor said. "I've wanted to come for a long time."

"I've never been here," she said with a laugh. "We should stay for a week or two."

"I wish," Kanen agreed with a smile. "But we have jobs to go back to. These guys came to help me out, and we can't take advantage of that."

"I'm so sorry," she said. "You're right. We'll make it as fast as possible." She pointed at the road sign up ahead. "And we're here."

They turned, following the GPS instructions per their rental car. Very quickly they pulled up by a small townhome with a Spanish-looking roof meshed between two other very similar-looking buildings. She hopped out and, with Kanen at her side, marched up to the front door and knocked.

It took a moment before an old man came to the door. and rapid-fire Spanish was shot at them.

When he stopped, she asked, "Do you speak English?"

He said, "Yes, I do. But why is it you think everybody should speak your language?"

She winced. Not exactly a good start. She studied his features and realized he, indeed, was the man in the photo. Although he might be a good fifteen to twenty years older. She pulled out a photo and introduced herself. "This came into my possession. I didn't know if it was important for you to have back."

He looked at the photo. His eyes widened, and a red wash of anger ripped up his features as he spat out Spanish in a deeply ugly tone.

Kanen stepped forward and held up his hand. "Stop."

The old man stared at him, almost vibrating with rage.

In a calm voice, Kanen said, "She had nothing to do with it. She's not part of the blackmail. Her husband, who is now dead, had a bag of these photos he was asked to keep for somebody. She wanted to return it to you. There are four more. She's happy to destroy them. But she didn't know if you wanted to know where the originals were."

As Kanen spoke, she watched the old man's features. Slowly they calmed as he realized they weren't here to extort money from him.

He took the photo from her hand. And then raised his eyes to Kanen's face. "There are more?"

She pulled out the envelope and handed it to him. "Five in all."

He took them from her fingers and shuffled through them, his shoulders sagging. "You had nothing to do with these?"

She shook her head. "No. The first I saw of them was earlier today."

He frowned and tapped the photos. "I paid a lot of money to get these."

"And you didn't get them?"

He shook his head. "I'd hoped to but no. And then I thought maybe they didn't exist and how I had paid for nothing," he admitted. "Now you show up with them decades later, and you're not looking for money?" Doubt filled his gaze as it went from one to the other, including the two men standing behind Kanen and Laysa.

She smiled up at him. "No. But, if these were photos of me, and I was being blackmailed, I would want the original photos back, even though digital copies or the photographic film from an older camera may still be available."

He nodded. "If there are digital copies, or the roll of film itself exists, then I still have to worry, don't I?"

"We don't know that there are digital copies or any film," Kanen interrupted. "We think the blackmailer, or somebody involved in the affair, held the originals as leverage against somebody. Maybe multiple somebodies, people like you. But, for some reason, he has now come back after the originals."

The old man thought about it, but he certainly wasn't slow. "The only reason he would need them is if he had no other copies and needed these originals." He nodded and pushed open the door. "I am Carlos. You may come in," he announced. He led them past a small parlor-type room and back farther to a large family kitchen that opened up to a small garden in the back.

He sat down on a bench in the backyard. "She's my wife, you know. At least she was after those photos were taken."

He looked at the photo, his fingers gently caressing the woman's features. "At this time she was married to someone else, but her husband passed away after being ill for a very long time. I was a politician, so, once he passed, we waited a decent amount of time, then married. But, since I was an upcoming politician, just before I was being voted in as a member of the parliament, these photos were sent to me, with a note saying they would be on the front page of every newspaper if I didn't pay. At the time it would have been terribly damaging to my career," he confessed. "She was fairly well-known, as was her husband, and very well-respected. Our images would have been forever tarnished."

"I'm sorry," Laysa said. "People are opportunists. And they will try to ruin our life sometimes, but we don't always have to let that happen."

He studied her face. "How did you get involved?"

She sat on the bench beside him and explained again how her husband had accepted something from a man who asked him to keep it, and her husband had died almost a year ago. When she came home to her apartment yesterday, she had been held captive for many hours. The stranger tried to find out where the bag was, and he beat her.

Carlos looked terrified at the concept of her being beaten, stared longer at the bruise on her jawline. He kept patting her knee, trying to console her.

She realized she had tears in the corner of her eyes. She

sniffed them back and smiled brightly. "It's okay. Kanen came to help. And he brought his friends. It didn't take long for them to find the photos. But we didn't know what they meant. Or what we were supposed to do with them. If these photos could be returned to their rightful owners, maybe they could have some peace of mind after all this time, and that's what I want to happen the most."

"You have a big heart," Carlos said with a smile. "Anja would have liked that." His gaze dropped to the photos in his gnarled fingers, still working over the surface. "She died five years ago, and a light went out of my world. The older I get, the more I realize the important things in life—whether you live five, ten or one hundred years—are really the relationships you make and keep throughout that life."

She studied his well-worn features, struck by the wisdom of his words. "I agree," she said softly, "because that's exactly what I feel now. Although I lost my husband, I'm so grateful I had the time I did with him."

He held up the photo for her. "You can't stop looking for another relationship," he announced. "Because, my Anja, she loved her first husband. Loved him very, very much. And though she was with me at the end of her time with him, it wasn't because she wanted to be disloyal. It was because she wanted somebody to care, somebody who would hold her, who would let her know it would be okay, even as she had to return to the dying man she loved. But it was a burden for her that she had nobody to share with. I was her friend. I became her confidant, her supporter and then finally her lover. We knew it was wrong, but we couldn't help ourselves from taking these stolen moments. Moments to help us return to the separate worlds we lived in.

"After her Andre died, I couldn't convince her to marry

me. She was so sure we had done something terribly wrong. It wasn't wrong," he said with strength, "but it took a long time to convince her. Finally I did, and together we honored Andre's life by being happy, by reliving the memories of him, by holding him in honor, by speaking about him, by keeping his legacy alive. We did many good things for the community in his name—set up scholarships, set up grants and programs. We did everything for him because it made us happy. He couldn't be here with her, but I'd like to think he was smiling from above, giving me permission to make her happy because he wasn't here to do so himself."

She was touched by that. "And I'm sure he did smile, that he would be happy to look down and to realize it was important for her to carry on and to have a good life too," she said with a smile.

The old man turned to look at her. "That goes for you as well. You cannot stay alone. You are young. You have your whole life ahead of you."

She chuckled. "I don't intend to stay alone. I was very upset, depressed, and I grieved for a long time." She smiled again. "But it's recently been brought to my attention that the time of mourning has come to an end. And it's time for me to face forward and not backward. I can carry the memory of Blake inside, but I can't carry his ghost any-more."

The old man nodded in understanding. "Good. You need to let it go." He held up the photos in his hand and said, "Even though these photos cost me a lot of pain and anger—and a lot of sleepless nights where I wondered what happened to them—I'm very grateful to have them now because they are of an Anja who I knew at the very beginning of our life together. And that Anja was a very, very special woman."

"I'm sorry they are so voyeuristic," Laysa said quietly. "Everybody should be entitled to privacy."

He smiled. "Anja would say that's very true. But she was never ashamed of her body or the joy that being together could bring. So, although she would be ashamed to have unknown people viewing these photos, and I can't imagine how many may have seen them over the years," he said sadly, "she would probably look at the photos, wince and then say, 'Carlos, I look good, don't I?'"

His words made Laysa laugh. "That is a great attitude," she said and stood. "We didn't want to disturb you. Thank you very much for giving us a few moments. We just wanted to let you know the photos are now yours. We don't believe any other physical copies are left, but we can never be sure."

Carlos waved a hand, as if dismissing the idea. "It is not an issue. I am old enough now that any pictures like these are just memories of a time when I was a younger, more virile man, with a woman I loved very much. They don't make me ashamed. They bring smiles to my face with the memories and maybe a little resentment that I have grown old and lost the one I love." Then he chuckled. "I will not pay blackmail again. It is a loser's game. And there's never any peace of mind, even once the payment is met."

Kanen nodded. "That's a very good lesson for everybody to learn. But we all have different reasons for paying off a blackmailer. It might very well have been because you didn't want anything to disturb your rise in politics." His voice was low but deep with understanding. "But I suspect it had nothing to do with that."

The old man turned to look at Kanen, his eyebrows lifting. "What is it you think I did it for?" he asked in challenge.

Kanen studied him and then smiled. "You did it to avoid embarrassing and humiliating and shaming the woman you loved. You would never have paid the blackmail against you alone, except for the pain it would have caused somebody else."

The old man smiled. "That is very true. I would have done anything to preserve Anja's peace of mind. I would never have wanted to humiliate or to shame her. I would never have wanted to shame her husband. They were good people, both of them. That they are now together in heaven is something that brings me peace."

Laysa held out her hand to shake his. "Thank you for seeing us. It makes me feel so much better. We came all the way from England just to hand these to you. But, more than that, I wanted to meet you. I wanted to give you that little peace of mind. Yet you didn't have to see us, and the anger you showed us in the beginning is what we had expected. But I'm really glad to know a much kinder man is on the inside." With that she turned and walked toward the front door, the men still gathered around Carlos.

He called out to her, "Wait. Don't you want to know anything about the blackmail payments?"

She stopped and gave a little gasp, noting the men had not moved. "I completely forgot." She rushed back to Carlos's side. "Do you know who blackmailed you? Was there any way to identify him?"

"Yes," he said. "It was an old colleague of mine. I used to meet him in the coffee shop and make the payments."

"So you know who he is?" Laysa asked.

He nodded. "I tried to kill him at the time. But, of course, that was much too much melodrama."

"Can you give us any information on him?"

The old man got up and walked into the kitchen, then over to a small desk. There he opened the top drawer and pulled out several photos. He handed them one picture, with him and another man. "This is him. I paid him cash for a year, and then I told him no more. He seemed to accept it, shrugged and said it was good for a while." And then Carlos stopped speaking.

"This man is too old to be the one who held me captive," Laysa said. "I don't understand …" She turned to look at Kanen. "How does any of this go together?"

He took the photo from her and studied it intently before handing it to Taylor and Nelson. "I don't know," he said, "but I can tell you one thing. It will connect. That's how this evil works. Somewhere it will make sense."

She looked at the other photos the old man had in his hands. "Who is in those photos?"

He sighed. "I had images of him, wanting to do something to destroy him, as he had threatened to destroy me. I could never go through with it. Joseph Carmel was his name. He had a wife who knew nothing of what he was doing, and he had a son who I knew would be forever harmed by the knowledge of his father being a criminal. So I did nothing. We had an uneasy truce for a long time. I think he knew, if he asked me for more money, I would do something serious to end his extortion. There is an art to understanding your prey, and I think he realized he'd reached my limits."

"Why do we have five photos of you? Did you get any from Carmel at the beginning?"

The old man nodded. "He gave me two. Both were worse than this." His voice went a little faint. "I think that's why it made me so mad, to think he was staring at my beautiful Anja without her permission, without any of us knowing. It was so wrong. And so very invasive."

"Did the blackmail last long?"

"No, no, no," he said, shaking his head. "After I said, *No more*, I just shut him down. We had an uneasy working relationship for another few months, and then he disappeared for years. Ironically he lives close by now, but I don't have anything to do with him." He slowly shook his head from side to side. "I haven't forgiven him for what he did, but I have moved on, just wanting to forget it all happened."

"I think that's what we all want," Laysa said starkly. "I want that man who beat me to disappear, so I never see him again."

"Is it possible Laysa's assailant is the blackmailer's son?" Taylor asked. "It would most logically be somebody who had access to the photos."

She looked to the old man. "Joseph Carmel, how old is he now?"

"Same age as me. Ninety-one."

"And Joseph's son. Do you know what his name was?"

He held up one of the photos. "This is his family. That's his wife and his son, Murray."

She took the photo and studied it. She looked up at Carlos. "May we take this with us?"

He nodded. "Take it. More bad memories I no longer want to have with me. Take them all. I hope you find whoever it was who did this to you. I don't want to ever hear any more about it. So, when you leave, please don't contact me again."

At the door she leaned over and impulsively kissed Carlos on the cheek. "Have a good life," she said.

He grabbed her hand as she walked away. "No," he said gently. "It's you who needs to make a new life for yourself.

My life is old, and it's done. But you—you have so much to live for. So remember. It's all worth living."

Then he stepped inside his house and closed the door while they watched.

"I think those were words to live by," Kanen said. He nudged her toward the vehicle. "Come on. Let's go."

"Where?" she asked, bewildered. "Time to return to England already?"

"No. Time to walk around and to create a few memories of our own," he said gently.

IT OCCURRED TO Kanen that he was walking a fine line. Blake had been his best friend. They'd been so damn close, almost brothers when they were younger. That had changed somewhat when Blake and Laysa connected but not enough to shift the core of their friendship. He'd been so happy for them when they had married. Kanen had never had his eyes on her, never been jealous of either of them. Since Blake's death, he'd done his best to be there for Laysa.

But now he also realized he might be interested in being there for her a little more—make that a lot more. And he struggled to come to terms with whether he was encroaching on Blake's property, crossing the friendship line or reading something into his relationship with Laysa that wasn't there anyway.

Obviously Kanen had been Blake's friend, but now Blake was gone, and Kanen was here. He thought about Taylor's and Nelson's words earlier. It was quite possible Blake would be happy for Kanen and Laysa to get together. That Blake would encourage Kanen to take the extra step to be with her. But he had to get over that feeling of Laysa being his best friend's wife and instead view her as a single woman on her own.

If he'd met any other widow or divorcée, Kanen never would have questioned it. But, because he knew the missing partner, had had a vast and deep relationship with Blake of his own, it made Kanen feel odd.

She squeezed his hand and said, "Penny?"

He chuckled. "It would take several pounds to drag it out of me."

She dipped into her pocket and pulled out a few crumpled bills. "How about this much?"

He shook his head. "No. Honestly I was thinking about Blake."

Startled, she looked at him. "Why? Do you think he was involved too?"

He hated to hear the suspicion in her voice, as if somehow Kanen would betray everything they had shared by believing something wrong about Blake. "No. He would never have been involved in blackmail. I have no misconceptions about who Blake was. He was a man's man, quick to judge and very quick to laugh. He would offer you the shirt off his back, if you needed it, but he also liked to be the best at everything," Kanen said seriously. "He had the best taste in friends and partners."

She chuckled at that.

Kanen smiled because he, of course, had intended her to.

She nodded. "He did, indeed. And you're right. He was quick to judge. But he was also quick to forgive. Although sometimes he didn't like to see anybody else's point of view, once you got him to consider it, he would admit he might not always be right."

Kanen agreed with that too. Blake had been a lot of

things. Kanen couldn't imagine Blake was terribly easy to live with because he had been fairly opinionated. Kanen could also see that, if a buddy had needed Blake to take care of this parcel, he wouldn't have thought anything of it. He would have stuck it in his gym locker and forgotten about it. "I guess I'm worried that his death had something to do with this," he said seriously.

"No, no, no," she cried out.

Taylor and Nelson looked over at him.

"We wondered when you would return to that," Nelson commented.

Kanen nodded slowly. "I didn't want to even contemplate it. Who does?"

"We're not going there," Laysa whispered. "It was hard enough to lose him. No way I want to consider that he was murdered."

"We don't know for sure that he was," Taylor was quick to point out. "Think about it though. It was almost a year ago. Was anything else happening in his life then?"

"Me," she snapped. "I was happening. We were arguing just before his death because I wanted to start a family, and he didn't." There was a note of bitterness in her tone.

After her miscarriage, Blake had said to Kanen, in private, how Blake had been relieved and wasn't sure he would ever be ready to have a family, not with his affinity for risk-taking hobbies.

And yet, Kanen could see that, for Laysa, this would be a big deal. Kanen had planned to visit them anyway and had come soon afterward. He'd held her for hours as she had grieved for her lost child, taking a week off from teaching, yet Blake continued working his job. She'd always wanted a family, a big family preferably, but would be content with just two children if that was all they could manage.

For the first time, Kanen wondered what would have happened down the road if neither would have been willing to budge on that major point.

Kanen frowned as they walked. They'd found the answers they came looking for in Spain. Of course that spawned many more questions, but, in the meantime, they had a free afternoon ahead of them. He wanted to walk through the village, to enjoy the sights, maybe to stop and have a coffee and a treat somewhere along the line. But now that they'd brought up this topic, and he knew it would be hard to come back from.

"Was there anything else happening to Blake at that time?" Nelson persisted. "We have to consider everything."

She shook her head. "I don't like this line of thinking. I get that you have to ask, but Blake wasn't the kind to get into trouble."

Kanen came to a stop at that. He turned to look at her. "That's not quite true."

She frowned up at him. "Since I met him—or rather, since we married—he'd stayed out of trouble," she corrected. "Although he still loved to live on the edge."

Kanen considered her face for a long moment. "That might be closer to the truth," he said. "But, in all the years I knew him, he was always in trouble. In the pub for a friendly drink, he'd always challenged the biggest guy. We ended up in more dustups for a lot of stupid reasons." A huge grin took over his face. "The Blake I knew, he was always happy to jump in and cause a ruckus, just for the joy of fighting."

"Right," she said, "but you know as well as I do that, in the year before we were married, he calmed down quite a bit."

"Quite a bit, yes. But I wonder what he was like at the gym."

Silence followed as she pondered that for a moment. And then shook her head. "I can't imagine it would be any different than what he always was. He was very steady, very stable with me."

"Of course. That's what you needed," Kanen said thoughtfully. "The thing that you really wanted was somebody you could count on. And he was determined to be that."

"There was a lot more to our relationship than that," she protested. "That's a very simplistic way of looking at our marriage."

"Not necessarily," he said. "We all have things we give and take in relationships, and, in this case, that was important to you. Your father had run off on you. Your mother used to take off all the time on you, even your brother did. And I remember you telling Blake very clearly that you wanted someone who would stay at your side, someone you didn't have to worry about deserting you." Kanen cupped her chin, lifting it ever-so-slightly. "Whether you like remembering that or not, it was definitely one of the rules of your relationship."

She tucked her chin down and walked several steps forward. He followed at a slightly slower pace. She hunched her shoulders. "Do you think I stifled the real him?"

"No," Kanen said gently. "I think he was happy to do it because it was important for him to be with you. You were everything to him. And he made a lot of changes for you because he wanted you to be as happy as he was," Kanen admitted.

He hadn't spent too much time thinking about it, but,

now that he was on the topic, Kanen could see how the relationship with Laysa had changed Blake, how he'd pulled back from so many of his rougher activities. He used to box in the ring just for fun. It was fitness for him. But then he loved nothing better than a good rowdy brawl. At one point, they'd contemplated joining a football team in the States, just for the physicality of it.

Of all the things Kanen had done with Blake, Kanen had never gone to the gym with Blake. Definitely not here in England. Never in the States either. *And that was interesting.* Because Kanen didn't know what Blake would be like in that environment. Kanen sighed. Blake was probably much more aggressive in a gym than in a bar fight because he was supposed to fight others there.

Kanen pulled out the gym manager's card and dialed Mark, while the others walked slowly forward, watching him. When the call was answered, he asked what Blake's behavior was like at the gym.

That drew Laysa closer to Kanen again, leaning in to hear Mark's side of the conversation.

"I knew him when we were younger," Kanen explained. "And Blake was quite a punch-up, dustup kind of guy. Always happy to jump into the fray and pound a few faces to the ground. Did he use the gym as an outlet for all that energy?"

The voice on the other end of the phone chuckled. "Absolutely. I had to get in his face a couple times to stop him from getting into everybody else's. We try hard to have a no-contest type of a gym, but gym junkies can be like that. *Who can pull the most weight? Who can bench press the most?* Everybody prides themselves on their upper body, whereas Blake was really, really strong in his lower body. He used to challenge people on lower-body competitions, so he could win. But he wasn't quite so gracious about upper-body competing because he knew he'd lose."

Kanen understood completely. "I wondered if that was the case. Did he ever get into any real fights with anyone?"

Mark's voice was thoughtful as he slowly replied, "A couple complaints were made against him. I had to, you know, like I said, get in his face a bit and have him calm down and back off. People come here to work out. They don't want to get stressed out by having someone else on their case. Every time I would talk to Blake, he'd calm down for a while, and then somebody would piss him off, and he'd go jump into it again."

"At any time was it to the point of him losing his membership? Was he ever that much of a disruptive force that you felt he couldn't come back?"

"Once I warned him that it was his last chance."

"When was that?"

"Not very long before he passed away, actually," Mark admitted. "He got into a ruckus with a bunch of the steadies here. Though Blake had been coming for a couple years, these guys had been coming for a decade plus. And they were pretty fed up with his attitude."

"How bad was it?

"It took all of us to break them up. I reviewed the tapes afterward, and it was obvious Blake had been pushing their buttons. So he got his final warning. If he'd done it again, he would have been out, never to return. He seemed to smarten up then. He apologized, saying he didn't know what got into him. He was just frustrated at home and needed an outlet."

At that Laysa turned her huge wounded eyes to Kanen.

"He was having trouble with his marriage. His wife

wanted to start a family or something, and he didn't want anything to do with that. She'd lost a baby once, and he'd been relieved. She wanted to try again, but that was the last thing he wanted. He was using the gym as a way to get away, a way to drive some of that temperament back inside again so it wouldn't spill over into his marriage. I told him that he couldn't just come here and beat up on other people because he wouldn't come clean with his wife."

"Your guilt kept you from opening his locker all this time, didn't it?"

"Yeah, I guess. It's not like I needed the locker. And every time I looked at it, it just kind of made me feel sad. I wish I'd done more."

"Done more ..."

"I have to admit. Every time I think about him, I wonder if he didn't commit suicide. Maybe things were so bad at home that he took a fast and easy way out."

CHAPTER 8

S *UICIDE?* CRUSHED, LAYSA took several faltering steps to the side of the road, where a short stone wall stood. She sat on top of it, collapsing, her mind reeling from the suggestion. It had never occurred to her. Why would it? As far as she'd known, they'd been blissfully happy. Blake was a great man. She refused to believe anything differently. So he hadn't been ready to start a family? That was hardly a character flaw.

But how happy could they have been if Blake would go to the gym, picking fights with other guys to work off some of that angry energy? That didn't sound like a happy guy to her at all. As a matter of fact, it didn't sound like a happy marriage either. He'd had a temper, ... but that's why he'd gone to the gym.

If she hadn't pushed him about having a baby, would he still be alive? She couldn't let that thought go. It just drilled deeper and deeper into her soul, splintering everything she thought she knew about their life together. She'd never questioned the police. They'd told her it was a car accident, and she'd believed them. She didn't remember the details now. She didn't want to know. They told her that he hadn't suffered, and that had been all she needed. She couldn't bear to hear how bad it might have been.

She presumed Kanen knew. Because he was the kind

who wanted details. She was pretty sure he'd said something about getting the rest of the information, and she'd said not to tell her. She'd wanted to remain in her happy little bubble that said Blake had died instantly and hadn't suffered.

She lifted her gaze to Kanen's hard face. He stared at her, a worried look in his eyes. "Is that what you found out from the police? That Blake committed suicide?"

He moved forward and dropped to his knees in front of her. He picked up her hands and held them close to his chest. "No. Suicide was never mentioned, was never contemplated. The evidence at the scene confirmed it was an accident." He paused, then added, "Just like the police said at the first and what I relayed to you."

She closed her eyes as a wave of relief washed through her. "I don't think I could stand it if he had committed suicide to avoid me," she whispered. "Even without him attempting suicide, here I thought we were happy, and instead he went to the gym to beat the crap out of people so he didn't come home and beat me up." She raised her gaze in bewilderment. "I never saw it in him."

"Good," Kanen said with a little more force than necessary. "Think about that. He did everything he could to let all that aggression out a long way away from you, so you didn't see it."

"But then what else didn't I see?" she asked quietly. She knew the other men were listening in. There was really no way to keep this private. But then they already knew so much about her that it didn't matter now. "Maybe he did know this guy? Maybe Blake *was* involved in the blackmail?" She stared at Kanen, her heart sad, her mind confused. "How do I know anymore, when everything I thought I knew wasn't real?"

"Everything you thought you knew about him hasn't changed," Kanen said. "Just because he goes to the gym to let off a little steam, that doesn't change who he was."

She had trouble believing that. They were in this absolutely beautiful little town in Spain. It was so unique and so quaint, and she'd never been happier than when she had stepped out into this area. Just to see the countryside, to see how different it was, wishing with all her heart Blake was with her.

And now she was out here with everything about Blake crumbling at her feet. Was she making too much of it? It just seemed like such an inherently big issue, a huge part of his personality, to have not understood that about him. Sure, people would say she was female, and he was male. They'd say all kinds of things, if they got a chance. But the real issue was the fact that she felt like he'd been hiding who he really was. And she didn't know what to do with that information.

Kanen stood, reached out a hand and said, "Come on. Let's go for a walk."

She shook her head. "I don't feel like it."

"Too bad." He snatched her hand and gently pulled her to her feet. "We'll head over there to that little family restaurant. I'm hungry."

"About time somebody mentioned food," Nelson said. The men seemed eager to have a change of topic. "That looks like a great place to sit down and have a bite."

She knew what they were trying to do. It was just hard to let them do it. She wanted to curl up in a hot bath and dive deeper into this issue, and they didn't want anything to do with it. Was that just another elementary difference between males and females? She couldn't believe how hard this one issue hit her. It was difficult to imagine how different she and Blake really were. It never occurred to her to go to a gym so she could get into a physical fight to expend energy before going home to her spouse.

What did she do when she got stressed?

She'd cry. She'd hit that point where she couldn't do anything about something, and she'd burst into tears. It was so unacceptable to Blake, probably as bad as his fighting was to her.

She always felt so much better afterward, and Blake always felt so much worse. He didn't understand how the crying was a release, how it was beneficial for her. Was that the same thing as the fighting for him? Was it a release? Was that how he felt when he was done? Did he not hurt afterward? She never hurt from crying. Her face might get puffy and hot, but she always felt so much better that it was an easy thing to deal with. She didn't ever remember him coming home with black eyes or a broken nose.

Then she frowned. That wasn't quite true. Several times he'd had some bruising. He just brushed it off. And she let him because she didn't want to know. If he said it was all good, then she was fine that it was all good. So why was it not all good now?

Because now it felt like a betrayal. And she knew she had to get her mind wrapped around that. If nothing else, she would pay better attention to her next relationship, would listen to the actual words—not ignoring the truths staring her in the face, not reading between the lines or thinking she could change the guy—and would open up more herself. She sighed, emotionally reeling that she hadn't learned to do that with Blake, the love of her life. Her soul mate. Her husband. Her friend. And possibly a man she barely knew inside.

She shook her head at those thoughts to keep her tears at

bay, bringing her back to this idyllic Spanish town.

She was tugged forward down the street to the small restaurant with tables and chairs outside, surrounded by a little iron gate. She took the seat in the corner with both Nelson and Taylor beside her. Kanen walked into the restaurant, returning to the table shortly.

Within minutes an older woman bustled out, an apron wrapped around her waist, delivering something that looked like coffee, only in a shrunken cup. It smelled like coffee, coffee on steroids, and Laysa wondered if it was a special kind of espresso. Menus were delivered too, before the woman left them.

Laysa picked one up, looked at the list of offerings and chuckled. "I don't understand Spanish. Does anybody else speak and read the language?"

Nelson nodded. The waitress returned soon afterward, and a rapid-fire exchange followed between Nelson and the waitress. When they were done, she collected the menus and disappeared inside.

Laysa stared at Nelson in surprise. "Wow. You did that easily."

He shrugged. "I was born and raised in Texas. Half of the population there speaks Spanish. The other half speaks English. Most of my friends spoke Spanish growing up. It was a pretty easy language to pick up when you were a kid."

She nodded and asked, "Are we having lunch or dinner?"

"It's after eleven o'clock," Taylor said. "And all we had was a little food on the plane. So I don't care what we call it as long as we get to eat."

She laughed. "So, in other words, you guys are seriously starving, and I—who never eats breakfast in the first place—

didn't even notice. Is that the idea?"

Nelson nodded and gave her a big grin. "You have no idea how happy I am that you finally decided we would eat."

She shook her head. "I didn't. Kanen did, and you could have said something at any time."

"And what? Slow the momentum of whatever it was we were doing case-wise? Oh, no," Nelson said. "I'm good. It comes from our navy training. Work comes first. We eat when we can. We sleep when we can. But now that we're at the restaurant, my stomach is screaming for joy."

She motioned at the menu and said, "Order me something small then."

At that, the men discussed whether they wanted pasta or pizza or something completely different. She wanted vegetables, something that she wasn't sure the guys were all that fond of. It seemed like a heavy meat-and-pasta dish would be the main order of the day.

When Kanen stood and returned the second time, he carried a basket of fresh breads. He set it down with a pot of what looked like whipped fresh butter. She realized she was hungrier than she'd thought. She reached for the first bun, and, after that, the basket emptied almost instantly.

She stared at the men as they almost breathed down the food, as if they hadn't eaten in days. "I guess I really should have said something about food earlier, shouldn't I?"

They all shrugged. "We could have waited a while longer," Taylor said in a boastful voice. "We're all good at starving when we need to. But, when there's food, you can be sure we'll make up for it."

She chuckled. It was such a joy to watch them as they ate. Blake had eaten well, but he hadn't eaten like this. And he'd gone to the gym and worked out. "So do you guys work out like Blake did?"

"To a certain extent, yes," Kanen said. "But never without control. We're there for fitness, not for muscles. We're there to make sure we're always in peak form before we get a call, so we're ready no matter what it is we must deal with."

Taylor lifted his phone just then and said, "There is a bit of good news, there's been no pings on our Ipswich hotel room."

"Good, that's what we like to hear," Kanen said with a nod.

Lunch was delivered within a few minutes. She looked down at her fresh-looking pasta covered in a white sauce and fresh herbs. Somewhere in there was chicken. She ate slowly, savoring the unique flavors. But the men didn't. They seemed to enjoy it just as much as she did, but they ate at twice the speed. And when the empty plates disappeared and came back refilled, she gasped. "You got seconds? Or did you have to reorder?"

They grinned. "She saw how hungry we were and took pity on us," Kanen said, batting his eyelashes at Laysa.

And that set the tone for the rest of the meal. Light-hearted joking and teasing ensued, and her melancholy and confusion were swept aside in the tide of good-naturedness. It was good to have friends like this. Good to have friends who took the time to change whatever was going on into something so much better. She sat back and nibbled on her first bun as the men worked their way through their second platefuls. "What are we doing now?"

"We're set to return to England tomorrow morning," Kanen said. "I highly suggest we act like tourists this afternoon, take in some of the sights, stop and have some wine somewhere. It'll be siesta time soon. A siesta is always good."

Taylor nodded. "Exactly, but a lot of food is consumed during that time too."

She shook her head. "No more food for me. Not until dinnertime."

At that, they pulled out their phones and checked out the local tourist sites.

Ending the silence as they all studied the screens on their phones, she asked no one in particular, "Should we be looking for the son?"

Taylor faced her with a sad smile. "I already did. He passed away two years ago."

She stared at him in surprise. "Really?"

He nodded. "Apparently he had cancer and didn't make it very long."

"So the son is not our home invader then," she said slowly. "What about the father?"

"He's alive and in a retirement home not very far from here," Taylor said. "We were wondering about stopping in to see him this afternoon."

"Is it open during siesta?"

They shrugged.

"It's not very far away. We can always pop in and say hi, if we're allowed," Kanen suggested. "If not, then we can do something else."

She nodded, took another bite of her bun and thought about the little they'd learned that morning. "Still makes you wonder who would care enough at this point to do something like this."

"And some of those photos are of no value—not from a blackmailing viewpoint," Nelson said. "Like Carlos said, he's no longer in parliament. So why hang on to them? Why not just burn them?"

"Because you don't know what could change. You just never know who might pay for something down the road, like a family member who doesn't want Grandpa's legacy soiled," Kanen said quietly, a frown growing on his forehead. "What if we're on a completely wrong track here?" He looked around the table. "What if this Joseph Carmel guy— the original blackmailer—just wants to publish a tell-all book? They seem damn popular. Everything from mommy issues to the size of some guy's privates or details about sexual proclivities appears to be the norm. Maybe this guy is dying and wants to write a book about his life and how he blackmailed all these people."

Silence took over their table as they shook their heads, contemplating a world where reality TV superseded movies for entertainment.

"But then who was the younger guy who broke into my apartment and beat me up?" Laysa asked.

"Could have been just an Ipswich street thug that Carmel hired online," Nelson offered. "Wouldn't be the first time we saw that happen."

"Or maybe," Laysa suggested, "Carmel's ashamed of what he did earlier, now that he's older, wiser. Now that the photos have been found, have resurfaced. Maybe discovered by a grandson or whoever. Maybe Joseph's trying to keep it out of the public eye?" she said.

"Again good guesses, but that's what they are, just guesses," Kanen said. "We might never know for sure. We'll talk to this Joseph and see what he has to say."

She stared out as the hot afternoon sun rose. In her mind there were too many options, but she could remember the desperation in her captor's voice, the anger as he beat her. As she thought about him hitting her, she thought about Blake and that temper he had obviously tried to work out in the gym. She remembered seeing the rippling of her captor's muscles. Her words blurted out. "I think my assailant went to the gym with Blake."

The men froze, turning to look at her.

"Why do you say that?" Nelson asked.

"He had the same hard muscled look as Blake, a similar look to the biceps and forearms. There was a real desperation in his blows. He wanted these photos in the worst way. He said it was his insurance. But who's to say exactly what his reasoning was."

"In which case we need to call Mark, check out who goes to Gold's gym."

"Especially at the same time that Blake worked out. Maybe my assailant was an old friend of Blake's. Maybe the asshole was somebody Blake met there. Although, if that's the case, why didn't the guy suspect Blake kept those photos in his gym locker?"

"Because, to the other guy, these photos were incredibly valuable. And nobody but a fool would keep them in a gym locker with no real security."

She nodded at that. "That makes a twisted kind of sense."

They got up, paid their bill and walked back to the rental car. As they drove past Carlos's home, she turned to look up at the old man's house. He stood in the window, watching them. She lifted a hand in greeting as they sped past. "I wonder what he's thinking about."

"Maybe nothing," Kanen said. "Wondering what kind of fools we are that we're chasing this now."

"Well, for me, it's not such a long time ago," she said

quietly. "That asshole was in my place just yesterday."

As a conversation stopper, it worked. Nobody said anything else as they drove to their hotel for their evening in Spain. Not long afterward, they all walked into their hotel suite. Two bedrooms and a central living room. Just like the guys' London suite. She had one bedroom to herself, and the men were all jammed in the other one.

Good, she thought. The last thing she wanted was any more contact with Kanen right now. She was just tired of the unpleasantness of the whole damn investigation. She had learned disturbing things about her marriage, about her husband. Still, they found no real answers as to who her assailant was and what was his motivation, just more questions. She threw herself down on the bed and closed her eyes. Siesta was a hell of a thing. And very quickly she fell asleep.

KANEN PACED THE living room of their suite. He'd called Mark, the gym manager, twice already, getting more information about men Blake seemed to hit it off with, not to argue with. Mark had come up with two names. Both Ipswich locals.

Kanen waited for Laysa to wake up, so he could ask her about them. But instinctively he figured she wouldn't know them or anything about them, not even their names. Blake had kept a lot of things separate from her, and this seemed like one of them. Possibly not on purpose but it appeared to be his way of having a life outside of their home and their marriage. An interesting mind-set for someone who was so invested in the marriage otherwise.

In a way it made sense because Blake wouldn't want to

be anything less than perfect in Laysa's eyes. He had such a complex about being the biggest and the best. He was one of those guys who would never dare back down—at least not easily.

It didn't mean he wasn't a nice guy because he was. It didn't mean he wasn't generous of heart and a great worker, because again, he was. But he had definitely kept a part of his life separate from his marriage, something Laysa didn't know about—until now. That ability to stay true to himself—even if just partially—must have made Blake feel good. Too bad he couldn't share that with his own wife.

Kanen would ask Laysa what she thought. He wished he could ask Blake what it truly did for him to keep that part of his life hidden. Keeping secrets was never good within any relationship. It usually was for selfish purposes, not for the good of both parties—whether in a business relationship or in a personal relationship. If secrets were kept, it was to do something the other person would not otherwise agree to.

Kanen threw himself into the living room chair, picked up his laptop once again and researched the two men Mark had given him names for. Just then his phone rang. It was Mark again. "Did you forget somebody?"

"Yeah, I did. Somebody from a couple years back," he said slowly. "I didn't think about him because I haven't seen him around in a long time. Blake was working out one day, when the guy stepped into the gym. Blake raced over and almost tackled the guy. He was so happy to see him. The other guy didn't appear to be anywhere near as happy to see Blake, though."

Kanen nodded. "Do you remember what this guy's name was?"

"No, I can't. I have hundreds of guys through here in

any given year."

"Does he have a membership?"

"No. He was a drop-in for a few months. He disappeared as suddenly as he appeared. I remember asking Blake about it once. He shrugged and said that was the kind of friend he was. He would just up and move to another part of the world. Something to do with his job, but Blake was sure the guy would drop in again. And sure enough he did. It wasn't all that long before Blake's death, I think," Mark said thoughtfully. "The trouble is, my memory is pretty wonky, since I've seen probably a total of a thousand or so guys in this gym. It's hard to keep track of them all."

"Any idea how close to Blake's death?"

"Nah, I don't remember. But they seemed to be buds still, and then, when he took off again, I didn't see him anymore."

"You haven't seen him since Blake's death, right?"

"Nope."

"Description?"

"Couldn't tell ya. I see so many guys coming through here. How am I to know this one would be important years later?"

Kanen nodded. "True. Any idea if they were friends in school, friends at work?"

"They talked about one of the local boxing clubs here," Mark said.

Kanen straightened. "Blake talked about one in particular a lot. Barney's, wasn't it?"

"Barney's, yeah, that's it. I heard Blake was really good too. Apparently they'd been in the ring together a time or two."

"And let me guess. If Blake was super friendly with him,

Blake won, right?"

Mark laughed. "I don't know, but it might explain the guy's expression when he saw Blake again. It was kind of a surly damn-it-what-are-you-doing-here type of look."

Kanen chuckled. "Yeah. Blake loved to win, and, when he did, he could be a bit of an egotist and in your face about it."

"Well, they got over it, so that's good." Mark cleared his throat. "You knew Blake well, didn't you?"

"We were friends for decades," Kanen said. "I knew the man as well as my own brother."

"I do remember something else. The guy who came in had a big nose, got it punched a couple times. Looked like it had been broken, set, then rebroken, and all of it badly."

"Dark skin tone?"

"Yeah, that's him. Do you know him?"

"I remember hearing about a guy with a big nose and something weird about his muscles. Blake used to laugh about him," Kanen said.

At that, Mark laughed. "That's the guy then. Because Blake was mocking him when he was here too."

After he finished on the phone, Kanen sat quietly for a long moment. Taylor and Nelson both looked at him.

"Your friend sounds like a complex character," Nelson said quietly.

Kanen's lips quirked. "That's one way to describe him."

"How does that help us now?" Taylor asked.

"I'll contact Mason to have him check with MI6 on the facial recognition issue." Kanen checked the time, realized it was early in the morning for Mason, but he was likely up. He dialed and waited until someone answered. Mason's voice was gruff, growly, but awake. "Too early to call?"

Kanen asked.

"Nah, I've been up for an hour," Mason said. "Just haven't had enough coffee yet."

Kanen laughed at that. "Neither have I. It's almost midafternoon. Doesn't look like a whole lot more coffee is coming my way either."

"What'd you find?"

Kanen filled him in on the old man living here in Spain and his history.

"Interesting but not really relevant."

"No. The blackmailer's son, Murray Carmel, is dead, so he can't be Laysa's assailant. Carlos's blackmailing colleague is Joseph Carmel, and we could stop in later today to see if he remembers anything or has anything to add. He's in an old folks' home up here and in his nineties now. Both the blackmailer and the blackmailee retired here in Spain but have nothing to do with each other. Laysa is having a siesta. It's been a rough day." Kanen hesitated, then said, "Did you hear anything from MI6 about the other photos?"

"They identified two of the remaining six unknown men in the photos. One was a big businessman, and one was a politician. Both have been contacted. Both admitted they did pay blackmail way back when. But it stopped relatively quickly, and they didn't do anything else about it. I'm sure they're worried those photos would come back up again."

Kanen didn't get it. "Why go to the trouble to catch people in embarrassing moments to blackmail them and then stop abruptly? That makes no sense."

"Exactly," Mason said. "These two guys didn't want to look a gift horse in the mouth, but, when it stopped, they kind of held their breaths. When nothing happened, they breathed again. They'd love to have the originals back, as they were shown copies in the first place."

"Hopefully MI6 will give them the originals," Kanen said. "What about the people in all the other photos?"

"Nothing MI6 was prepared to share at this time." Mason's tone was dry. "But you know what that's like."

And Kanen did know. It was all on a need-to-know basis. Generally he never needed to know. He was one of the workers, one of the guys who fought for the world and didn't understand the orders given from the brass above.

"Will talk to MI6 when we get back from the old folks' home." Kanen disconnected the call and looked up to see Laysa standing in the doorway. Her arms were crossed over her chest, and she looked tired. He hopped to his feet and wrapped his arms around her. "How are you doing?"

She gave him a tremulous smile. "I'm better. Still tired but how much of that is emotional, I don't know. I forgot about the old guy Carmel. Let's go see him now, then have dinner. An early night and an early flight would be good."

"We can change the fights and leave tonight if you want," Taylor said. "I doubt it would cost very much."

Startled, she looked at him. "Really?"

He nodded. "If that's what you want to do, we can make it happen."

She appeared to think about it and then shrugged. "We're in Spain, and we might as well at least enjoy one night." She smiled at the others. "Although I might change my mind after I talk to the old guy."

Everybody laughed.

"Before I forget ..." Kanen asked her about the three men from the gym who Mark had singled out, but she shook her head.

"I don't know any of them."

He held out a hand. "If you're ready to go then …"

She smiled, placed her hand in his and said, "You know me. I'll follow you anywhere."

As they walked out of the building and headed across town, still within walking distance, she wondered at her words because she had followed Blake everywhere. Was that what she was thinking here? Was she subconsciously exchanging the two men in her mind? Because that would never do. Yet so much history was shared between her and Kanen that what she'd said made sense. It was still strange. And she kind of worried he thought something of it that she hadn't intended. But it was hard to tell. At least her voice had been low enough that the other men hadn't heard because that would just add to the awkwardness. Something she didn't want.

Outside, she stopped and took a deep breath. It was a sultry, hot afternoon, but the sun was a little bit behind the clouds, giving her a breather from the dead heat.

At a good pace they headed toward the old folks' home. "Good thing Nelson speaks Spanish. It's benefited us before. And it may help us a lot when we get there."

Nelson smiled. "Why, thank you, Laysa. It's nice to be appreciated. Maybe you'll rub off on these guys."

That brought laughter from everyone, even Nelson.

"Leave it to Nelson to add some humor to our days," Kanen noted.

As they approached the front entrance, she looked at the tall two-story almost-cathedral-looking building. "It's a pretty nice place to spend your final years," she murmured.

"Maybe," Kanen said. "Not sure that any of these people would agree with that. It seems a far cry from the life they used to live."

"But their lives have changed now," she said softly. "I think most have come to accept this is where they are. Although it probably took some time to make that adjustment, ultimately I'd like to think they're happy."

He patted her hand. "That's because you believe in the fairy tale," he said. "The happily ever after."

She frowned. "That makes me sound like I'm unrealistic or some Pollyanna," she said. "Like I have no spunk, no spirit."

"Not at all," Kanen said, shaking his head. "You're a spitfire by day—a scrappy fighter when needed—and a romantic by night. ... Kind of like Blake maybe?"

She frowned. "*Hmm.*" She studied Kanen for a couple minutes. But she was thinking about Blake and Kanen's words. "Maybe."

"Now you're not alone. You've got friends here to help you."

"Ha. Until you leave."

The sad note in her voice was unmistakable. "You don't need to *remain* alone. That choice is up to you."

They opened the double doors and walked into a front reception area that rivaled any grand hotel.

She stopped and smiled, gasping at the big chandelier and the large circular desk. "This is beautiful," she murmured.

The woman looked up from the reception desk and smiled. "Thank you. It was an old estate handed over to the city for the seniors to use."

"I approve. And I love your accent. You speak English very well," Laysa said with a smile. "It's a beautiful place to spend your retirement years."

"Thank you. Most of us speak English here," the receptionist said with a gracious smile. "What can we do for you?"

Kanen stepped forward and gave Joseph Carmel's name.

The receptionist nodded. "He doesn't get many visitors," she said, "and none from England or the States."

Laysa just smiled at her. "Is it a problem to see him? We'd like to very much."

The woman nodded, looked at a computer screen, clicked on his name and said, "He should be in the gardens this afternoon. Either there or he'll be playing cards." She gave them general instructions on how to reach the gardens.

They thanked her and walked away. And, sure enough, several older men were outside.

Laysa frowned. "How are we supposed to know which one is him?"

Kanen smiled, motioned to a nurse in a white uniform and said, "I suggest we ask."

Before he had the words out of his mouth, Nelson had walked over to the closest staff member and had done just that. The nurse turned slowly, surveyed the people out in the garden, then pointed to one man standing by the roses. Nelson thanked her with a big smile and motioned in the direction of the older man.

They walked slowly, not wanting to engulf him. When they got closer, the older guy turned and frowned. Kanen stepped forward and introduced himself in English.

The old man shook his hand and then looked at Laysa. "And who is this lovely young lady?

Laysa smiled and introduced herself. "We have a few questions we'd like to ask."

Nelson stepped forward, adding, "About blackmail years ago."

Joseph slowly sank into his wheelchair parked beside

him. He turned to Nelson and said, "If you would push me back to my room, I'd appreciate it."

Kanen stepped forward. "Will you talk with us?"

Joseph looked up at him. It was easy to see he was visibly upset. "There isn't anything to say. I lost a colleague—a man who I would have liked to have called a friend—but for my actions."

"So why did you do it?"

"Because I didn't want him to get the position I wanted," the old man said. "I can't believe this has come back up again. It was over and done with a long time ago."

"But you were never charged, were you?"

The color swept out of Joseph's skin, leaving him pasty-faced. "No. And, at this point, I wouldn't survive a trial. I have to meet my maker over my actions. Isn't that punishment enough?"

Laysa didn't think so, but then it was kind of hard to know what his maker would really say to him. "Somebody had a lot of photos. He said it was his insurance policy. That's how we came to find them. Do you have any idea who would be in possession of these photos now?"

His gaze widened. "No. I have no idea. I'd hoped they had all been destroyed by now."

"Did you take some of the photographs originally?"

He shook his head. "No. I only took two of the prints. And I used them to get money from my colleague," he said painfully. "I've paid for that decision for the remainder of my life. Everything went wrong from that moment on. I lost my wife, and I lost my son. I sit here all alone."

"Where did you get the photos?"

His lower lip trembling, he said, "Honestly, a bag was at a bus stop one day. I sat beside it and noticed the photos inside. Nobody seemed to be around, so I picked out a couple to look at. They were of my friend. We were friends at the time," he explained. "I wanted to get a closer look at the rest of the photos, but a man came rushing toward me and snatched the bag. I didn't see his face. What he didn't know was I still had two photographs in my hand."

"And you used those photos to blackmail your colleague, correct?"

The old man nodded. "That's correct, although that was a long time ago. I'd hoped the world would have forgotten it all by now. I've regretted it ever since."

"How old was that man who took the bag and ran?"

He frowned. "He was young, very young."

"And he didn't explain where he got the photos?"

The old man shook his head. "But he had camera equipment with him, so they were probably his photos. I can't be sure, of course, but I think he was the one taking these terrible photos."

"And you just used his work and blackmailed your friend." Kanen looked at the old man in disgust. "And how many other photos do you think were in that bag?"

Joseph stared, belligerence in his eyes. "I don't know. Hundreds likely."

The four looked at each other.

Laysa turned and, over her shoulder, said, "Thank you for the information you gave us."

"Wait. I know the name of the company."

She spun on her heels. "What company?"

"The photographer's company. It was all over the bag." Joseph smiled in triumph. "It was Finest Photos," he said with a big grin. "Finest Photos, Ltd. See if you can find that after all these years."

CHAPTER 9

A S SOON AS they walked away from the strange older man, Laysa half whispered under her breath, "Find that company."

"Right," Nelson said in an odd tone. "How does that help us?"

"We should have asked him if that was on the back of the photos," Taylor suggested. "What's the chance that was the mark we saw rubbed off?"

"If that's the case, then it is important," Kanen said.

"That may be," Taylor said, "but that doesn't give us the answers we need."

"But we won't know until we take a look," Nelson replied.

"We also didn't ask him if he knew where the company was located," Laysa noted. "Or anything else about it."

"He wasn't too cooperative at that point anyway," Kanen said in a comforting voice. "We can find that kind of information on our own."

"Can we?" she asked.

"Sure," Kanen said. "We just need access to the internet."

Taylor pulled out his phone, checked it and said, "I've got bars. Give me a few minutes, and I can track down something on that company."

They walked in silence back toward the hotel. It was hard not to appreciate the beauty of their unique surroundings. The cobblestone streets absolutely amazed her with how well they fit together. She understood craftsmen did this day in and day out, but this road had to be hundreds of years old, and yet, it was still in remarkable condition. There was a ruddy, rusty red color to it that just added to the amazing color around them. The hotels and buildings alongside the road were in various bright, cheerful colors. It made her smile inside and made her forget those other thoughts in her mind for a bit.

The sun was still high, and some of the clouds whispered past, adding to the postcard-perfect picture all around her. She gave a happy sigh, plunging her hands into her pockets as she walked beside the men. "This isn't exactly how I thought to come to Spain, but I'm so happy I finally got here," she murmured.

Kanen silently wrapped an arm around her shoulders and tucked her up close.

It was pretty hard to not enjoy the moment. Being close like this, her heart against his, the warmth of his body washing over hers, ... it was ... perfect. Did he feel the same way? Then he said something that surprised her, and it let her know maybe, ... just maybe, ... he did.

"Sometimes we just take the moments when they happen," Kanen said.

Suddenly Taylor stopped. "Well, look at that. It's a British company. It had offices all across Europe way back when. They were big-time."

"*Were?*"

Taylor nodded. "Closed down in 1995, from the looks of it."

"And their stock?" Kanen asked.

Taylor gave a shrug. "Who can tell? Have to do a little more research to figure out how and why they closed. Was it the death of the owner? Was it a business going under? Was it rendered obsolete in this digital age?"

"That probably wasn't widespread until the year 2000 or so," Nelson stated.

Taylor nodded and continued, "Of course the real evolution in photography came with the advance of cell phones with camera features—which again began around the year 2000 as well. Sure people still had Nikons and SLRs, but every Joe Blow could take decent photos with their cell phone."

Kanen agreed. "Then the photography business went under. Along with the video rental businesses and many others."

Taylor and Nelson nodded in agreement.

Taylor waggled his phone. "I'll let Mason know. See if he can find anything on Finest Photos."

"Sounds good. A restaurant is up ahead. Are you ready to eat?" Kanen asked everyone. He pointed to an outdoor café, just starting to fill with people.

She smiled in delight. "Oh, yes," she said warmly. "I could really go for some nice vegetables."

The men snickered.

"You can have your vegetables. We'll go for the meat," Nelson said.

"You need to have vegetables too," she scolded with a groan.

"Oh, don't worry," Taylor said. "We will have plenty of vegetables. But we'll get plenty of meat too."

An hour later—after a bread course, a soup course, a

salad course—they were seated in front of gleaming plates heaped high, hers full of sautéed vegetables with some cheesy sauce over the top and a small piece of salmon beside it. She looked at the salmon and smiled. "Seems strange to eat salmon here. Like, don't they have any local fish from this region?"

"Sure, but they also take pride in having the best of everything," Kanen said.

As she looked at his big platter of steak, steamed vegetables and one of the largest baked potatoes she'd ever seen in her life, she shook her head. "How can you possibly eat that much?"

He patted his tummy and smiled. "Easy. Just watch me."

Dinner was an enjoyable affair as they all tucked into that good food and a great bottle of red wine she'd never tasted before and couldn't begin to pronounce. She took a picture of the label in case she could find it back home.

Just as they were sipping the last of their wine over empty dinner plates, Taylor's phone rang. He checked it and held up a finger. "It's Mason."

With the phone to his ear, he spoke in a quiet voice, so she could barely hear. She waited until he was done.

He hung up and looked around at the group. "There was quite a scandal before Finest Photos closed—the owner, one of the Alagarth family members, went to jail for blackmail."

"Seriously?" Laysa asked. "Isn't that a little too easy?"

They laughed.

"We never get easy cases," Kanen said. "Don't knock it when it actually happens. It's probably the only time in the next ten years we'll get something that's easily solved."

"I don't think it'll be quite so easily solved," Taylor said, typing away on his phone. "Alagarth got out of jail after four years. He'd been protesting his innocence the entire time, and, within weeks of his release from jail, he was murdered."

Laysa stared at him. "So he was innocent, goes to jail for a crime he didn't commit, and, when he comes out, the guy who did the crime shoots him?"

"Don't know about any shooting," he said. "I just have news he was murdered. We'll have to dig up the old reports to see how he was killed."

Kanen pointed a finger at her and said, "And that is because you were thinking it was way too easy."

The others all gave sage nods.

And she glared at them. Then, in a mocking voice, she said, "I think you guys just enjoy that this challenge continues. You all want to have this kind of drama in your lives."

Kanen's eyebrows shot up. "Not likely." He waggled his eyebrows. "I can think of much better things to spend my time on."

She snorted.

Taylor hopped up and said, "I don't know about you guys, but I'd like to get back to the hotel and do more research on my computer instead of reading my tiny phone screen. Anything we can find before we return to England could make a big difference."

"Is Mason still looking into Finest Photos too?" Laysa asked.

Taylor nodded. "To a certain extent, yes. But he is heading out on an op and won't be back for four days." He glanced over at the other two. "A trip we're missing, by the way. He's heading up to the Yukon."

"Dammit, we're missing all the fun," Nelson said.

Taylor just chuckled. "Yeah, we're missing the Yukon

horseflies, heat and mosquitoes. While we're sitting here in Spain in the sunshine, drinking great wines and enjoying wonderful meals."

The other two considered that, then nodded.

"Good point."

On that note they returned to their hotel room, where Laysa headed to the jetted bathtub, while the men sat down with their laptops open. The last thing she heard was their discussion about the method of the murder and the black-mailer's guilt or innocence.

After her bath, she dressed, feeling one hundred times better, and stepped into the living room. "Did you guys find anything?" she asked, towel-drying her hair.

The men smiled up at her.

Kanen chuckled and patted the seat beside him. "Come and take a seat. I'll show you what I found."

She collapsed beside him, and he placed a laptop on her lap.

"We have copies of his court case, what was released for public viewing anyway. And we have a copy of the coroner's report on his death. No autopsy was done. He was shot, one bullet between the eyes."

She looked at him. "And does that mean anything?"

"It could mean many things. That's the problem. It could mean somebody close to him shot him. It could mean it was a sharpshooter, like a sniper. It could mean somebody with a pistol had a good aim. It could also mean somebody held the gun against his head and just fired."

"It still seems very sad," she said. "If he spent years in jail for a crime he didn't commit, it would have made him a very bitter person inside. He was probably motivated enough upon his release to come after the person he thought might have done this to him."

"But why would the real blackmailer kill this guy? The case was solved in the eyes of the court and the police. It was a done deal. The guy in jail had probably been hollering about his innocence for years now. Who would listen to him now?" Kanen paused, then raised his pointer finger. "Unless the guy released from jail had some proof. If he had that, likely the confrontation ended with the real blackmailer now being a murderer."

"Was anybody ever charged with his murder?" she asked.

"No. The case went cold and is, to this day, unsolved."

KANEN AGREED WITH her totally. But how did one find a murderer from an old crime like that? He sat back and contemplated their options. "The best place to start might be to find out all we can about the owner of Finest Photos. About his family, those closest to him back then. If he had any close business associates, female companions, or, if he was gay, a male companion. The murder itself wasn't difficult to enact, so either sex could have shot him."

She stared at Kanen in surprise. "Why is it I never even thought the original blackmailer could be a woman?" she asked. "Because that makes total sense. No way in hell she would go to jail. So it was much better to set him up."

That made the men laugh.

"Watch out for her, Kanen," Nelson said. "She'll make sure you go to jail before her."

Laysa shrugged. "I can't imagine either of us ending up in jail. Now you on the other hand ..." she said with an evil grin. "Somebody might just blame you for something, and you'll find yourself behind bars."

He gave her a mock look of fear.

She rolled her eyes and went back to the laptop. "So we need to know all of the above information, plus his personal relationships. Did he have any family? Maybe he has a brother he was in business with. Maybe something else was going on," she said.

"He had a brother and a son," Taylor announced from his laptop. "Heavily involved in the business, both of them. Disappeared from public eye after the sentencing. Then it's tough on the remaining family members when someone is jailed. Although, in this case, he protested his innocence constantly—apparently."

"What about names?" Laysa asked. "Same last names, different names, any grandchildren? The guy who accosted me in my own place would be younger, I presume."

"How young?" Nelson asked.

"Anywhere from twenty-five to forty-five," she admitted. "I know that's not very definitive, but it's hard to tell when the guy wore a mask."

"Close enough. It gives us a range," Taylor said quietly. "The owner's wife died while he was in prison. She had heart issues. Seems the son married, had a son."

"We have Grandpa Alagarth, who was killed, a brother who is potentially alive, a son who is alive, and a grandson who is alive, correct?" Kanen asked. "What are their ages?"

"Give me a minute." Taylor tapped away. "Okay. Give me more than minute. I'll get back to you on that."

"Or," Nelson offered, "I'll take over finding the DOBs. You handle Kanen's next questions." Nelson grinned like he was getting the better end of this deal.

Kanen had a notepad opened up on his laptop as he jotted down the family tree. "What about the brother? Did he have a wife? Several wives? Kids, grandkids?"

"Definitely could have," Taylor murmured, typing while he talked. "Not sure anybody beyond the brother is applicable though. The relevance here is, if the brother was heavily involved in the business, he could have been the blackmailer. Nobody would have known he would have used the business as a front, and his brother could have been completely in the dark about it all. Then again, that goes for all the employees as well."

"How much did the sale of the businesses net?" Kanen asked.

"Several million," Taylor said. "I've just lost the page. Hang on while I go back."

"Even though he was charged and convicted of blackmail?" Laysa asked.

Taylor nodded. "He had multiple stores across Europe, a great franchise. It brought in multiple millions. Ten point four million," he announced when he found the page.

"So," Nelson theorized, "what if the grandfather didn't get any of that blackmail money? What if it went to the grandfather's brother and the grandfather's son? When Grandpa gets out of prison, he wanted his share, and they weren't willing to give it to him."

"Conjecture all the way," Kanen said with a light tone of voice, "but I like it."

"The thing is," Taylor added, "we have to track down these people and go from conjecture to reality."

Laysa nodded. "Does anybody have any photos?" she asked of the men. "It's not like I saw my captor's face because he wore a full ski mask, but I certainly saw his body type. Although I guess that can change from generation to generation too, can't it?"

"Absolutely," the men said.

"I don't think photographs would help much. It would probably just confuse you all that much more," Taylor said.

She nodded. "Kind of depressing to think he was there in my apartment for hours, and yet, I couldn't identify him."

"No tattoos? Nothing distinct?"

"No, just like I said, it looked like he was a bit of a gym junkie. Very rip-cord, bulging-veins type of guy. You know what I mean." She looked at the other men's wrists, but they all looked normal. "None of you have anything even close to his, so it's hard to explain." Then she opened up a new tab on the laptop and compared images of bodybuilders and different lean-muscled men, looking specifically for their wrists and their forearms. She found one that was similar. "Like this," she said, holding up the laptop. The men studied the image that showed ropy veins and tendons and muscles up to the biceps.

They nodded. "Yeah, we've seen something like that on guys—gym rats—before."

"But this guy was definitely extreme. His hands were thick, muscled and had zero fat on them. A darker skin tone on his arms too."

"And he had very little body fat all over?" Nelson asked.

"As far as I could tell, yes," she said. "He had on a muscle shirt and jeans and a knitted ski mask. So I couldn't really see much."

"You gave us his basic body mass and his height. I can extrapolate his weight," Taylor said. "There was nothing identifying in the jeans or the shoes?"

"Blue jeans. I couldn't tell you if they were designer or cowboy," she said with a laugh. "And he wore sneakers. That's all I can remember."

"Any idea what kind of sneakers?"

She shook her head. "No, but his feet weren't very big. Maybe because he wasn't terribly tall. Blake wore a size eleven shoe. But this guy's feet were much smaller than that. Maybe an eight or nine. But they were wide," she said as an afterthought. "Oddly enough, they were really wide."

Kanen jotted down the little bits of detail. "All of it helps. When we finally get our man, we can confirm some of the things you saw against our suspect."

"I just don't want you to dismiss anybody who doesn't have a really wide foot," she said, "because what if my memory is wrong? I was extremely stressed, terrified, in fact. And it's very possible I made a mistake. Plus my definition of 'wide' may not be your definition of 'wide.'"

"Which is why we'll keep it in mind," Nelson said. "But we won't take it as gospel."

She beamed at him. "You really are a very nice man."

He glanced at her in surprise and smiled. "Thank you."

Taylor looked at her and frowned. "Hey, what about me?"

She laughed. "You are too."

Kanen frowned. "So you mentioned my buddies as being nice guys, and you don't say anything about me? … *Sheesh.*" He grinned at her, letting her know he had no hard feelings.

It was nice she got along so well with the guys. He knew from them that they admired her guts. But, more than that, they also liked her. She'd shown herself to be somebody they could not only admire but who would fit in with the other guys in their units. A roomful of alpha males would never scare her off.

She leaned over and kissed Kanen on the cheek. "You're much nicer than a nice person. You're special."

At that, the men, including Kanen, went off on a bout of laughter.

She glared at them. "Now what are you laughing about, Kanen?"

He just chuckled, wrapped his arm around her shoulders, a habit he was doing more and more often. It was almost as if he wasn't comfortable or happy if she wasn't in his arms. "They expect the next thing out of your mouth to be an insult," he said. "Don't worry about it. They're used to being teased and to teasing each other."

She sighed and returned to the laptop in front of her.

He checked the time and found it was after nine o'clock already.

"We have an early morning flight," he said, "so the earlier to bed, the better."

She nodded. "Not an issue. But maybe, if you don't mind, may I check my email?"

"Sure, go ahead," he said. "You've got the laptop. You can do what you want."

She smiled her thanks, brought up her email program and flicked through it.

He searched the living room for what needed to be packed. They were good at leaving in an instant, so he wasn't worried they would need much time.

He heard the small gasp in the back of her throat and saw the color leach from her face. "Laysa, what's the matter?"

She swallowed hard and said in a faint voice, "*There's* an email I wasn't expecting." She closed her eyes, took a deep breath.

He squeezed her shoulder gently. "Hey. It's okay. What's the matter?"

She stared up at him.

The other men looked at her, waiting for her to gather her thoughts and to tell them what was going on.

"So, is it good news or bad news?" Kanen asked.

She took a deep breath. "I haven't opened it yet." She stared down at her fingers drifting across the email.

He didn't want to look because it was her confidential email, but, at the same time, he wanted to know what she was thinking. "Are you going to share?"

She lifted her troubled gaze his way and then switched to look at the other two men. "I just don't understand how this could have happened."

"If you don't explain it to us," Kanen said gently, "we can't explain it to you."

She nodded, took a deep breath and turned the laptop toward him, tapped the edge of one email, not opening it but letting him know it was there.

He stopped and stared. He raised his gaze and looked at it again.

She nodded her head slowly.

He faced the other two men. "This email is from her dead husband."

CHAPTER 10

L AYSA STARED AT the email. "How can this be?"
The others gathered behind her. "There's a good chance somebody hacked your husband's email account," Nelson said. "It's guaranteed to have shock value. And that's what you just had—a shock."

"It's also possible to set up an email like that before you die," Taylor said. "I know you don't want to consider that, but Blake may have sent it to you himself."

"But why now?" Kanen studied the email. He sat closer beside her, the laptop on both their laps. They hadn't opened the email yet but just stared at the bold lettering, showing it was an unopened email. "Is it from his usual account?"

"Yes," she said. "His work email."

"That would be much easier for somebody else to get a hold of then," Taylor said. "The naming convention at a job will be the same for each employee."

She understood what he was saying, but it was still rather unnerving. She clicked the email and opened it. It showed a picture of her standing almost nude in a bedroom. It wasn't her bedroom.

"Do you recognize that picture?" Kanen asked softly. He rubbed her shoulders, trying to reassure her that everything was okay. Or at least it would end up that way.

But she felt like she'd gone down a rabbit hole and didn't know how to get back out. "I don't know when this could have been taken," she said. "I'm not even sure where this is."

"And the next question is, why would somebody send it to you?"

She started to shake. "I swear I've never been in that bedroom. I don't recognize the wallpaper. I don't recognize anything about that room."

"Maybe it was altered via Photoshop," Taylor said. "Some pretty sophisticated Photoshop gurus are out there. They could have taken a picture of your head, attached it to a nude body and stuck it in somebody else's bedroom."

She twisted in surprise. "Could they really do that?"

"Absolutely. They can even add a date stamp." He pointed to the far corner.

"It's dated the day after I escaped," she said slowly. "I don't even remember if I had changed clothes that day. Things were a bit hectic."

Kanen asked, "Is there any chance this isn't your back?"

She frowned, thinking about it. "I guess there's one way to know. Here." She sat forward on the edge of the couch and lifted her shirt so the men could see her back. "You guys tell me. Is it?"

There was silence while they studied her back, noting some bruising—which Kanen felt better about not mentioning to her—and then the image in front of them.

"It doesn't have this mole here," Kanen said, gently placing a finger on the side of her spine.

"What does that mean?"

"Your back is also a little fleshier than the back in the photo," Nelson said. "The person in the photo has very low body mass."

She frowned, thinking about that. "I'm certainly not fat, but you're right. My ribs don't show."

"Thankfully," Kanen said smoothly. He tugged her shirt back into place. "So we now know it's not your back."

"If it's my head, you're saying they could have taken it off another photo and put in on this one?"

"Yes, exactly," Kanen said. "It's pretty easy these days to do something like that."

"But for what purpose?" she asked, staring at the photo. "I do have leggings like that." She tapped the bright blue geometric pattern beneath the skirt the woman held in front of her. "I rarely walk around without a bra. And this woman isn't wearing one."

"Again that could have been done with Photoshop software." Kanen studied the photo, then said, "It's not even that great of a job." He pointed out where the two middle sections of her body supposedly joined. Ever-so-slightly they were off. "It's hard to see here, but, if we opened this up in Photoshop, we'd see that discrepancy very quickly."

She sighed with relief. "I have to admit. I'm much happier to think this is a fake photo than to consider somebody took images of me when I changed."

"It's a warning," Kanen announced. "Basically telling you to stop what you're doing, or images of you will show up somewhere you don't want them to."

She turned and looked at the men. "And just what the devil do they think that'll do?"

Kanen shrugged. "The whole point of the photo will be to maximize your humiliation and to expose you. And again, in this case, it's blackmail of a warning nature. Not because they want money but because they want you to stop doing something."

"What we need to know though is who may have sent this to you," Nelson said. "Outside of the image, is there a message?"

She returned to the email. "No, it was sent directly from Blake's account at work," she said slowly. "There doesn't appear to be any other information on it." There was still a sense of violation as she looked at it though. Even though she knew it wasn't her back, she felt weird to think that not only had somebody manipulated her image to the point that other people would think it was her but that somebody was doing this to hurt her. "There has to be a way to find out who sent this."

"Anybody could have sent it if they worked where your husband did, or, if a good-enough hacker, could remotely get into his email account at work," Taylor explained.

"Sure, but he's been dead for almost a year," she said.

"It's still possible," Taylor continued. "After his death the company had to keep the email address working in case they needed to respond to people with current orders or to have Blake's replacement deal with his unfinished orders or to refer back to any customers he worked with and maybe special orders or special pricing. So his email account will be there, but it's probably been retired, maybe with one of those automatic vacation responders, telling people trying to reach Blake to now contact John Doe at his direct email address. So anybody in the company, or anybody who understood how email programs work, would have no trouble accessing it."

She sagged onto the couch. "It's an ugly world we live in."

Kanen's hand squeezed her shoulder. "That it is. We can

get Tesla to look into it, if she's available. She's a software designer and maybe can trace this or at least tell us she hit a dead end. But this is a relatively innocent email."

"*Sure*," she announced. "My dead husband sends me an email to my personal email account with a seminude photo of me, supposedly, and an unspoken message that appears to be very threatening. How innocent can you get?" There was no humor in her tone.

"Time for bed," Kanen said. "We are getting up early in the morning."

She handed him the laptop and stood up without a question. "I'm definitely tired. Maybe if I read something, I can take my mind off this." She smiled at the others. "Good night." She walked into her bedroom and closed the door.

THE MEN TURNED toward Kanen.

He shrugged. "What can I say? Somebody now knows she's on to them. That's the most concerning part of all this."

The others nodded.

"Agreed," Nelson said. "So we have to figure out who and how, based on our investigation so far."

"We'll be back in London tomorrow," Kanen said. "What I want to do tonight is gather as much info as we can on all the Finest Photos' owners and family members who may be involved, see if anybody is still alive and where they're working and living—especially where they were this last week." He nodded at Taylor. "Maybe the younger generations have social media accounts to help with that."

Kanen's voice hardened. "That asshole physically attacked her, and now someone's mentally working on her.

What if they forward that Photoshop email to her school? Or even worse, to her students? She'd lose her job while we gathered the evidence to disprove this. We've got to put a stop to this before somebody decides to escalate it even past losing her job and chooses to take her out of the picture altogether."

"I don't think gathering any more information on these people will help," Nelson warned. "We'll do it, of course, but the bottom line is someone—a single someone most likely—has a purpose for what he is doing. It won't likely involve anyone else. I mean, her attacker seemed to be working alone. This has all the hallmarks of a vendetta. A very personal one. Think of that asshole's anger as he beat Laysa when he couldn't find what he was looking for, no matter how many times she said she didn't know what he was talking about."

"We need to track him down," Kanen said, "and fast."

"Or set a trap," Taylor suggested, "but not until we know more."

Just then a text message came through. "Update from Mason. *Still running down names*," Kanen read out loud. "*Nothing popping so far. Not from our end or from MI6. Keep your heads down and stay safe. Sounds like you've got a lone wolf out there.*" Kanen raised a grim face to the others.

"There you have it." Taylor nodded.

Nelson said, "Mason's right. It goes along with what I was saying. All this Finest Photos blackmail and related events happened so long ago, but—for someone—it's still current. And he's on a rampage to accomplish something. And it doesn't make sense that he would go the blackmail route after so many years, decades even, have passed. So we have to figure out what his angle is."

"He's passionate about his goal. And willing to go over the edge to achieve it," Taylor added.

"As long as that doesn't mean coming after Laysa again." Kanen wanted Laysa safe at all costs.

CHAPTER 11

LANDING IN ENGLAND the next morning was a big relief. So much was going on, and yet, she had no closure. Laysa wanted the routine of her own life—although the thought of living in her apartment made her cringe now. She'd taken the week off from work, but that was soon running out. She didn't know if she could take off any more time without them replacing her. And that was disturbing in its own right. She'd miss the kids, ... and she needed the income.

If something happened to her, would anybody care outside of Kanen? Her parents were dead; she had no siblings. After Blake's death, she'd had no contact with his family, which had been sparse at best. And that was sad too. It was like all these strings had been cut from her life, and now she felt suspended, on her own two feet, but as if she were alone on an island and didn't really have any way to connect with the rest of the world. She hadn't isolated herself as much as she had allowed herself to be isolated.

On the taxi ride home, Kanen asked her, "Are you okay? You're awfully quiet."

She smiled up at him. "Just realizing how much my world has shrunk. With Blake's death, it changed the dynamics of my life in so many ways. Losing him was the epicenter of even more aftershocks radiating outward. I lost friends we had together, which shows me my girlfriends at the time were more couple-friends. I have hardly kept in touch with any of them. Blake was never close with his family, and we were never close to them when we were married. Now that I'm on my own, it's like a huge chunk of my life doesn't exist anymore."

There wasn't anything Kanen could say to that. Taylor and Nelson shared a grim look.

They got out at her apartment building, and she stared up at it. "Do you think it's safe?"

"Let's find out," Kanen said. "When are you supposed to return to work?"

"I told them that I was sick," she said, "that I would be taking off a full week. So I'm scheduled to return Thursday next week. I don't know if taking off like that'll get me into trouble or not."

"Are you still working at the same preschool?"

She nodded. "Yes, but they could easily replace me if I wasn't there. And missing a week of work at the beginning of the first semester of the new school year is not a way to endear myself to the school administrators or to the children's parents. I'm suddenly realizing that I'm really not important to anyone. And that feels very lonely."

"That's wrong," Kanen said. "You're very important to me."

She squeezed his fingers. "Yes, but, when you return to the US, you'll go back to your job and forget all about me. Yes, we'll talk on the phone a couple times a week for maybe a month. But it's not like you'll be there for me all the time, like these past few days. Any more than I would expect you to be." She paused, embarrassed, as she looked at each of the guys. "I know I'm whining. Just ignore me." She was calm, though, at the same time, her heart ached at the thought of losing Kanen.

"So come back to the States with me," Kanen said. "Nothing is keeping you here now, is there?"

A smirk appeared on Nelson's face. A *told you so* look.

Taylor lifted one eyebrow and tilted his head in a silent nod, agreeing with Nelson.

She stared at Kanen. "My apartment." Even though she'd said it, she shook her head. "I have some friends here." She spoke slowly, then stopped. "No, ... nothing is keeping me here." Her voice was low, almost in a dumbfounded way. "I'm not sure I like that."

"What? That nothing is keeping you here?"

"I don't like the reminder of how empty my life has become. When Blake was alive, my life was full. We used to have dinners with other couples. We did things as a couple. We biked, hiked and grabbed books and coffee to sit out in the middle of nowhere and just enjoy being together. Our lives were busy. But now it's just me. All that connected to his life has been removed, and I realize how much of it was part of *his* life. It wasn't *our* lives as much as it was *his* life."

"No," Kanen corrected softly. "When a twosome, you had other twosomes to connect with. As a single person, those couples don't know how to act around you. They don't know what to say to you any longer, how to fill up that empty space at a dining room table. And it makes them feel awkward to invite you over. So they don't."

She nodded.

The guys and Laysa got out of the cab in front of her Ipswich apartment.

"We should be allowed back in, right?" she asked softly. It didn't look like home anymore. Her assailant had tainted that.

"Of course. It's your apartment. It wasn't cordoned off before we left. Shouldn't be now," Nelson said, looking at his silent phone. "I'm surprised MI6 hasn't tagged us yet. Somebody should have been pinged that we're back in the UK."

As they walked to the elevator, she asked, "Do you think we should ask anybody?"

"You mean, ask MI6 for permission to enter your own apartment?" Taylor asked. "Hell no. I tried to get answers earlier from MI6 on other matters. I didn't get very far."

Now at her apartment door, she unlocked it and pushed it open. There was no sign of anyone having been here.

Regardless, the guys spread out and did a quick search just to be sure.

She walked into her bedroom, dumped her travel bags on her bed and said, "Doesn't look any different." She walked back out to the kitchen, where she put on a pot of coffee.

While she waited for it to brew, she looked around her apartment. It was an empty shell and symbolized so much of her life. Nothing was on the kitchen counters, except the coffeemaker. She had no toaster, no blender, nothing. She had put it all away after Blake's death because she didn't use them anymore. She rarely ate bread herself, and she hadn't ever baked anything here. She didn't care if she had a cookie or a cake ever, whereas Blake had loved his sweets. They had routinely visited a nearby bakery so he could get his sugar fix.

She walked back into the living room and sat down. She booted her laptop up and waited for it to load. "What's next on the list?" she asked.

"What do you want to do?" Nelson asked. "I can't say I

had enough to eat on the plane, and we didn't have breakfast before we left because it was such an early flight. So food right now wouldn't be a bad idea."

She chuckled. "There's the kitchen. Help yourself." She expected him to give her an argument, but he didn't.

He hopped up and walked into the kitchen, checking out her fridge and the cabinets. "You've got eggs. Do you have any bread?"

"Nope, I sure don't," she answered.

He rummaged a bit more, poked his head around the corner and said, "Do you mind if I make pancakes?"

She turned to face him in surprise. "Sure. Absolutely. If there's enough to make some for everybody, that's a great idea." She smiled as he puttered around in the kitchen. She looked at Taylor. "Do you cook too?"

"I can," he said. "Don't have much call for it in my world. I tend to do barbecues more than anything."

She nodded in understanding. "Men gravitate more to outdoor barbecues."

"Men gravitate to protein," Kanen said with a chuckle. "Big fat steaks."

"Well, you won't find any steaks in my fridge," she said, "but, if Nelson can make pancakes for all of us, that's perfect." Even the thought of it made her mouth water. She hadn't had homemade pancakes in a long time.

Before long, they all sat around her small kitchen table, enjoying a wonderful breakfast. She smiled at Nelson. "You can cook for me anytime."

He chuckled. "You're welcome at my table anytime too," he said with gentlemanly politeness.

She smiled and snagged another pancake off the stack. "These are really good. Blake used to make pancakes."

"Man food," Kanen said. "Something to stick to the ribs."

She nodded. "He often said stuff like that too." She waited a few minutes, while the men continued to eat. Then she asked, "How long can you stay in England?"

"Another two days," Kanen said. "I can stay longer if need be, if we haven't found this guy. But I can't stay too much longer."

She nodded. "I'd hate to be here alone if he hasn't been caught."

"Which is why," Kanen said, "you should come back with me."

"You mean, *run away?*" she asked, working up her face in distaste.

"Staying alive to fight another day," he corrected.

"Blake never ran away from anything," she said slowly. "I can hardly run away myself. Particularly if something is odd about his death."

"We're a long way away from having any proof of that," Kanen said. "Honestly I wouldn't go down that pathway at all. It's just going to twist you up inside."

She nodded. "I understand, but ..."

"Did you want to pull that thread?" Kanen asked, watching her expression change. "Just tell me if you decide you want more facts, and we'll see what we can do."

She nodded, her mouth a grimace.

As the men finished the pancakes, she rinsed the dishes before loading them in the dishwasher. "What's next then?"

"We'll contact MI6," Kanen said. "Make sure they share whatever information they may have found on those photos. Then we'll continue our research to see if we can track down any Alagarth family member still alive or anybody who knows about Finest Photos and what happened to them."

"A historian? A genealogist? ... Selfies on social media?" she quipped with a roll of her eyes.

"There are all kinds of choices," Kanen said. "In a way, MI6 might even be the best option, if they'll cooperate with us." He got up from the table, filled his cup with coffee. "I'll be in the living room, seeing if I can get a hold of anyone on a weekend."

It *was* Saturday. Maybe nobody would answer. In the living room she heard Kanen speaking to somebody. She continued washing up, and they all half listened to the conversation.

Finally Kanen came back in and said, "Well, I got them on the phone. Surprise, surprise. And they're still tracking down a few other unknown people in the photos. They did come up with a couple more. One is dead, and the other one is in a coma from a car accident he had a long time ago. The family has been fighting the courts not to take him off life support."

"Interesting. Do we think the death of one and the accident of another are related?"

"I doubt it. Seems the death was natural and much more recent," Kanen said. "These photos were likely blackmail material from years ago. I think our best bet is to track down the couple known family members of the jailed alleged blackmailer. They have the best motivation for wanting the pictures back."

"But what motivation?" she asked in bewilderment. She snagged a tea towel and dried her hands. "I get that there has to be some reason why they are important to someone, but it seems like the actual blackmailing itself is no longer viable."

"I think MI6 is coming to that same conclusion," Kanen

said. "That's why we should find the rest of the people in this alleged blackmailer's family. You look to those closest to the victim or to the perpetrator of the crime, usually family members. If somebody knows about these photos, somebody has a reason for wanting to hang on to them. And usually that is to use them as threats. To stop somebody from doing something. We still have to get to the bottom of the who, what, how and why."

After she finished cleaning up the kitchen, they sat around the table with their laptops, searching and making phone calls as they tried to track down the last few living members of the alleged blackmailer's family.

Kanen got another text from Mason.

It's possible the Alagarth family moved to the US after the grandfather was convicted. We have proof the son was in Maine for a few years. But the grandson appears to have returned to England.

We'll look for him. Kanen read his message as he typed it into his phone for the others' benefit. **We need to write him off as part of this or put him on the plus side and keep him as a suspect.**

Pressing Send, Kanen said, "That means the grandson is likely still here in England. Why is it we haven't found him yet?"

"Because we were looking for a Robert Alagarth. I suspect he's using the name Bob instead," Nelson said. "Because we found several Bob Alagarths. One in London working as a photographer."

"Are we thinking the grandson followed in the grandfather's footsteps?" she asked. "Are we also thinking he's a blackmailer?"

"No way to know. I suggest we pay him a visit," Kanen

said.

"I'm up for it," Laysa said. "If he's even there on a Saturday."

Next thing she knew, Nelson was making a call. "Yes, I wanted to stop in this afternoon but didn't know how long you were open." He smiled. "Thank you. We should make it." He hung up the phone. "They're open until five o'clock today."

She marveled at how quickly they got things done. They had been moving nonstop since arriving in England, accomplishing a lot on their list, even though not yet at the finish line. Before she knew it, the men had already set up a plan of places to go. They had two more Bob Alagarths who they considered viable suspects. Once they were packed up and ready to go again, she looked around her apartment wistfully, wondering when she'd get a full day to herself to just sit and do nothing, without a care in the world.

Kanen wrapped an arm around her shoulders. "You ready?"

She nodded and followed them out of the apartment.

They went to see the first Bob Alagarth on their list, the closest one to her apartment. They walked up to his flat and met him; he was probably in his late seventies. Definitely not the person they were looking for.

They carried on to the second one on the list. He appeared to be the right age, but it couldn't be him; ... he was black.

With that suspect crossed off the list, they headed to the photography shop. "What's the chance this is our guy?" she asked.

"As good as any," Kanen said cheerfully. "The question is whether you'll recognize him when you see him."

"It will be interesting to see his reaction when he sees her. So, take as much time as you need to recognize him and to take a good long look at him," Taylor said as they got out of the vehicle parked outside the shop, "I want to track this guy's reaction. That'll be as telling as anything."

They walked into the photography shop. It was bigger than she'd expected. "He seems to be doing quite well for himself here."

The shelves were full of lenses, cameras, supplies and other accessories. They wandered the store for a long moment, looking for the one person they were searching for. Two women worked at the counters.

Laysa walked up to one and asked, "Is Bob here?"

"He's in the back room. Did you have an appointment with him?"

She smiled. "We called and said we'd be coming. If it's possible, it'd be nice to talk to him."

The woman headed toward the offices in back. Because of what Taylor had said, Laysa stepped back behind the men. No reason for this guy to recognize Taylor or Nelson. He might recognize Kanen if he was tracking him through England's airports. But the guy would definitely recognize her if he saw her in the store.

The woman quickly returned. "He'll be out in a minute."

The men nodded and wandered the store. She deliberately kept herself hidden behind everybody, wondering if this Bob Alagarth could possibly be her assailant.

Soon a man in a business suit stepped forward, a bright smile on his face, asking the men what he could help them with.

That voice ... She studied the owner and realized she

couldn't tell just from that if it was him or not. She looked at his wrists, and, sure enough, he had the same ropy muscled arms as her captor, but was it really him? There was only one way to find out. She stepped forward into the middle of the men, smiled up at him and said, "There you are. We finally found you."

KANEN JOLTED AT her wording. He immediately turned to the man, looking for the response that would trigger a conviction one way or the other.

Bob swallowed hard and said, "I don't know anything about you."

She gave him a hard smile. "And that just convinced me even more. Your voice caught my attention first. You should have some scratches along your right shoulder." She immediately smacked him hard where she'd scratched him before.

He took a step back, glanced at the men and bolted.

The women in the shop screamed as Kanen jumped over the counter and raced after Bob. Kanen didn't waste time worrying about Laysa because he knew one of his two men would stay with her, the other right behind Kanen.

Bob disappeared into the back offices and out the rear exit. As Kanen blasted out the door of the building, he saw a small blue car already turning from the parking lot onto the road. The vehicle was older, more of a patchwork kind of a blue, as if different parts were taken from multiple vehicles of all different colors. It would be very hard to hide that vehicle. Kanen came to a gasping stop, furious to think this guy had gotten away from them.

Taylor stopped by his side, glaring down the road. Then he turned to him. "Are you sure that's him?"

They both studied the rest of the parking lot, looking to see if they spotted anyone else.

"It's just as likely he could have gone off on foot, using that vehicle's exit as a distraction." Taylor motioned inside. "If you want to check with the staff, I'll keep looking around out here."

Kanen returned inside and asked one of the staff what kind of vehicle the owner drove.

"He's rebuilding a small blue car," she said in confusion. "What's happened? What's he done?"

He pulled the woman gently outside to the parking lot. "Is his vehicle here?"

"Oh, you can't miss it," she said. "It's a wreck. It's got various bits and pieces that he's using until the parts he wants come in. And, no, it's not here."

Sadly that confirmed what Kanen had already assumed—they'd lost him. "We need a way to contact him. Do you have his phone number, his home address?"

But the staff member got irritated. "Hey, I don't know who you are or what you're doing here, but, if he took off, he had a good reason."

Kanen wasn't about to let her get away with that. But he didn't have to because suddenly Laysa was there in front of them.

She snapped at the woman. "Oh, he had a reason all right," she yelled. "He broke into my apartment, held me captive there and beat me up because I didn't know where his precious *stuff* was. Turned out to be blackmail photos."

The staff member took several steps back, her hand going to her chest. "That's not possible. He's a good guy."

But Laysa was pretty damn convincing as she explained what had happened. "See this bruise on my jaw where he planted his fist? More photos like this are on file with the police department, if you care to check."

The woman backed up another step.

"We've been hunting *Bob* ever since he attacked me. I'm still sporting his other bruises and have a few scars from the rough treatment he gave me." She spoke bitterly. "But I recognized him, both his voice and his arms. And I have no doubt that's who he is. He's the one who took off. Remember?" she snapped at the woman, getting the better of her again.

Kanen gently rubbed her shoulder. "We'll catch him, now that we know who he is and where he works. The police will nab him."

The woman stared at them in horror. "But I've known him for ten years. He'd never have done something like that."

"Maybe not before," Laysa said, "but he certainly did now. So we need to know what you know about him."

But the woman wasn't willing to cooperate. She stormed back inside.

Laysa followed her and started taking pictures of the store with her phone, Kanen right behind her.

The other staff member came over and said, "You can't be here. We don't know what the hell's going on, but we trust our boss."

Kanen nodded. "You can trust your boss all you want. But we're staying right here until the cops arrive."

"And MI6," Laysa said in a hard voice. "If you think they're not involved in my finding my assailant, you're wrong."

The women looked at each other nervously and then went back to their jobs.

Kanen didn't blame them. They had jobs to do, problems with their boss or not. "You might want to contact the higher-up boss if you have one," he offered helpfully.

The woman shrugged and said, "Bob owns the company."

"Then you better be looking for another job," Laysa said, "because he's going to jail for B&E, battery and extortion. Maybe even murder."

The women shook their heads and remained quiet.

Kanen had to admire that kind of blind loyalty, if that was what it was. More than likely it was a case of they didn't know what else to do. And he could understand that too. It wasn't like they'd given the women any warning or proof.

At that thought, he noticed the framed photographs on the side wall that Laysa was taking snapshots of. He pointed them out to the guys. One by one they studied these black-and-white pictures. They appeared to be of old photography stores.

"What's the chance these are Bob Alagarth's grandfather's stores? What if this is about revenge? About his grandfather's wrongful incarceration?" Kanen glanced over at one of the women. "Did your boss's father ever come into this store?"

The woman looked up at him nervously and shook her head, then went back to her work.

"Given his likely age," Nelson offered, "chances are he has nothing to do with his father's business, Grandpa Alagarth's chain of European stores. And, if Father Alagarth is still living in the States since about 1994, then he never was involved with his son's subsequent business either."

"So why did the grandson want that package from Blake?" Kanen asked in a low voice. "Unless he's trying to protect someone."

It was just too much for Laysa. She walked over to the closest chair, pulled it far away from the women and sat down. "How long before the police get here?"

"We called MI6," Kanen said. "They'll be here first." And, sure enough, he looked up to see two men in suits striding in the front door.

Their hard gazes searched the store. They came toward him with a strong determination that wouldn't be swayed. Neither of the women who worked at the store spoke.

Kanen explained what had happened. The men in suits took notes and then, when questions were completed, Kanen, Laysa, Nelson and Taylor were escorted from the store. Outside on the sidewalk, it dawned on Kanen. "Surely you'll do a full investigation?"

"Of course," one of the MI6 men said. "But we want to get our hands on him first. The store is just that. ... It's a store. It's nothing more than that."

"No, there you're wrong," Laysa said. "The history of the Alagarth family business is on the walls. The grandfather was wrongfully accused of blackmail, jailed, murdered. His assailant was Bob, the grandson and owner of his own photography store, this one. Those photos on the walls inside are interesting as far as the backstory of the family."

One of the agents turned to look at the double glass entrance doors. With a few quiet words to the other man, he headed back inside, as if to look at the photographs.

Laysa looked up at Kanen. "He needs to pull them off the wall, all of them, and take them in for evidence."

Kanen chuckled and tugged her a little closer. "They know how to do their jobs. Besides, they aren't really evidence. They are mementos of this guy's history."

"No," she argued. "They are evidence of his motivation. And that counts." She shoved her fists into her pockets and glared up at the men.

They stared back at her with calm, bland faces, knowing it was best to not say much at this moment, without getting into an argument with her. "Come on. Let's go back to your place," he said quietly. "We'll get the details soon."

She resisted but finally gave in. As she turned to walk away, she looked back at the two MI6 men and said, "Please catch Bob before he comes after me again. He beat me up and threatened to kill me."

The look on the agents' faces eased, and one of them nodded. "We plan on it."

As they walked toward the car, she turned to Kanen. "It's not fair. Bob was right there. He was so damn close."

"It would have been nice if you had pointed that out to one of us, instead of antagonizing Bob right off the bat," Kanen said gently. "We could have set a trap for him. As it was, he had the advantage of a familiar location and a clean line out of the building and a vehicle to run away in."

"I know," she said. "I didn't think. I'm sorry. Once I was convinced it was him, I confronted him to get confirmation."

Now in their rented vehicle, they headed toward her apartment. Kanen was a little worried. She kept staring out the window listlessly, as if Bob's getaway was all her fault. He slid his fingers through hers. "It's okay. We'll get him."

She nodded but didn't answer. Outside her apartment, she looked up at the windows. "It doesn't even feel like home anymore."

"Once this is all over," Nelson said with forced cheerfulness, "it will feel different, hopefully better."

She followed Taylor through the front doors. Kanen brought up the rear. He stopped to look around the streets. As long as her assailant, this Bob Alagarth, was loose and on the run, Kanen didn't dare leave her side. This Bob guy was just as likely to run to the main continent, but, if he was angry or wanted to put a stop to this, he might easily come back after her again.

Kanen stepped inside. As the rest of them entered the elevator, he said, "I'll take the stairs." He waited until the door shut and headed to the stairwell. He ran up the stairs quickly. On the third floor, he got out and walked toward her apartment. There was no sign of her.

He walked back to the elevator and saw it hadn't made it to the third floor, stopping on the floor below. Swearing profusely, he bolted back down to the second floor and came out of the stairwell ready for a fight, only to see the three of them talking softly outside the elevator. He came to a dead stop in front of them and reminded himself not to yell. "Jesus! I thought something had happened. What's wrong?"

She turned to him and raised both hands in frustration. "I don't want to go home."

He reached for her hands. "Then we don't have to go back there," he said quietly. "If you're nervous, or if you think something is wrong, if your instincts are telling you that you can't go there, then that's fine. We'll go to my hotel for the night."

He heard a heavy sigh and watched the relief cross her face. He enveloped her with a hug and held her close. "Look. You had a traumatic event in your apartment," he said quietly. "Of course you don't want to be there. Just say so. We won't force you to do anything. We're here to help keep you safe and to catch this asshole Bob. But let's not make fear be the reason you do anything."

She nodded and squeezed his back. "I know. I feel like we should avoid my apartment. I know I'm being foolish, but, at the same time, knowing that guy's out there ..."

"Which is exactly why the three of us are here with you," he said. "Now do you want to go back and make sure everything's okay? Will you feel better if you see that your place is the same as it always was?"

She tilted her head to the side as if contemplating that idea, then nodded. "Yes, I will."

They went back to the elevator, but she balked at the doors.

"No, I don't want to get in the elevator."

The other men exchanged worried glances, but Kanen grabbed her hand and said, "The stairs are fine."

They walked up the last flight to her apartment. There she unlocked the door, and Kanen pushed it open and entered. While they waited outside, he did a quick search of the entire place, ending his search in the bedroom, even checking under the bed and in the closet.

He walked back out to where they waited. "It's empty. No one's here. Come on in."

She walked in slowly.

He wasn't sure why it bothered her this time versus the last time, but he had to respect her feelings.

She stopped and pointed at the couch. "That is new."

Kanen inspected her couch, pulling out a note stuck between the cushions. He showed it to Nelson and Taylor.

"What does it say?" she asked.

"It'll be okay," Kanen began. "It seems Bob stopped by here while MI6 questioned us. He left a note saying, *I'll be back.*" He grabbed Laysa's shoulders. "We won't let him get to you again."

She nodded, trying not to focus on those three words.

"Hey," Kanen said, sucking her out of her thoughts. "You called it. You followed your instincts."

She nodded.

"No, really. You followed your instincts. It was a good call. Continue doing that. Always let us know when you have these gut checks, okay?"

She remained silent, still nodding her head as if unable to stop.

"Okay?" he asked louder.

"Yes." She smiled a weak grin. "Yes," she said in a stronger voice. "It scared me."

"As he meant for you to be," Kanen said.

"But I'm getting madder as I think about it."

Kanen and the other guys laughed. "You got it, Laysa. Turn that fear into fight mode." She'd gone through a horrible ordeal, and Kanen could well imagine she no longer had a feeling of home here. He'd be more than happy to take her home with him. All she had to do was agree. They'd been friends since forever. And she was definitely pulling at his heartstrings.

Now that Blake was gone, he shouldn't feel guilty about his feelings. It would take a little time to adjust to seeing her as someone in his life, not just as Blake's wife and as a longtime friend. He glanced at her, realizing it wouldn't take any time at all. He was almost there now.

She sat on the far end of the couch—opposite from where Bob's note was found—and stared up at Kanen, a wistful smile crossing her face. "It would have been so nice to have seen you before all this," she said. "Now it feels like we're not equals anymore."

At her odd wording, he sat down beside her. "We've always been equals. What do you mean?"

"I feel like I need you to protect me right now, and that makes me less than what I was before."

He shook his head. "That's so not true. We all need help sometimes. Even SEALs need help. Right now you need us. And that's fine. You might not need us tomorrow. You might not need us next week, but, for the moment, you need our help, and that's what we're here for. It doesn't make you any less in our eyes. In fact, I admire somebody who can accept the help when it's required."

She chuckled. "I forgot what a cheerleader you always were."

"I am what I am," he said with a lopsided grin. "And I have to admit that, right now, I am hungry."

She stared at him. "No way. You can't always be so hungry."

He shrugged. "Why not? It's got to be at least lunchtime, if not dinnertime. I've lost track of the time of day."

She snorted. "Well, if anyone wants to make something, go ahead, but I don't think I have enough food to feed all of us."

Nelson jumped to his feet. "Challenge accepted." He raced into the kitchen, with Taylor right behind him, both of them laughing.

She looked over at Kanen and smiled. "I like your friends."

He leaned over and kissed her gently on the lips, whispering, "They like you too."

CHAPTER 12

L AYSA WAS SURPRISED at the kiss, and yet, why should she be? They'd been heading toward this since he'd arrived to help her. She looped her arms around his neck and kissed him back. "I like you too," she whispered.

He settled her into his lap, and they sat here, cuddling. She thought about how long it had been since she'd been held by somebody who really cared and realized it had been way too long. "I've missed this," she announced quietly.

He looked down at her. "What?"

"Being touched," she said softly. "Cuddling. Just being with somebody who cares. After Blake died, it seemed like my world collapsed. I was so alone, like walking through a constant dark, cold night. And there would never be any sunshine ever again. Of course, eventually you pass through that phase, and you stare outside, and you start to reconnect with the world around you. But you're single now. There isn't anybody to hold you in the middle of the night when you had a bad day or a nightmare. There isn't anybody to pick up the phone and call or to send a happy face text to in the middle of the day just because you were thinking of them. Everything is geared for a two-person world, and, all of a sudden, you are cut in half. It feels so foreign, so strange and, most of all, so very cold."

He hugged her gently. She rested against his big chest.

She'd never thought of him as anything more than a good friend, … until recently. At the same time, she wondered why not. He was incredibly sexy, one of those strong and capable kinds of guys who oozed power and charm at the same time. She knew he'd had lots of girlfriends, but nobody he ever got close to.

She leaned back slightly, looking up at him. "Why did you never marry?"

He jokingly said, "Well, I could say because you were already married."

She wrinkled her face up at him. "No. I mean, why did you never marry?"

"Because I never met anybody I cared enough about to make it permanent," he said calmly.

She had to wonder at that. And his initial joke. Was this the time to ask him about that?

Just then Taylor poked his head around the corner, saw the two of them together and smiled. "Now that's much better," he said, "to see the two of you like that."

She raised an eyebrow. "Ha. You don't know anything about us."

He shrugged. "And? That doesn't change anything, does it? Not really. But the reason I'm here is to ask if you had any plans for some of the stuff in your freezer, or can we help ourselves to whatever we need?"

She waved a hand at him. "I doubt much is in there. Have at anything you want."

Kanen called out, "It's better if we use up everything anyway. She won't be staying here, so the less to move, the better."

Taylor gave a big nod with a happy grin. "Got it." He disappeared again.

She leaned back and turned to look at Kanen. "What are you talking about?"

"You don't want to be here. You don't really have a job you can't live without. You're all alone. And you just said it's like a half life. The dark half. I want you to come stay with me," he said. "California is warm and sunny. Leave the rain here. I have a two-bedroom apartment, so plenty of room, and I think you could make a new life for yourself there."

"I'm not a charity case," she warned.

He snorted. "Nobody in their right mind would call you a charity case." He tilted her chin up. "Is that why you keep ignoring me when I ask you to come home with me?" He studied her a moment, but she kept silent. "Can you look me in the eye and tell me that you really want to stay here all on your own?"

She winced. She tried to pull her chin away, but he wouldn't let her. She glared up at him. "I don't know what I want."

His gaze warmed.

She sighed and smiled up at him. "You're right. I don't want to be here alone. The invasion of my home and the beating was enough of an experience, without factoring in the loss of Blake, so I don't want to stay in this apartment. But moving back to the US is a big step."

"You moved here with Blake, but California has always been your home. Is there any reason you don't want to go back home?"

"It doesn't feel like home," she said. "Even though I lived there for so long, it doesn't feel like going *home*."

"Good point," he said. "But does this place feel like home anymore?"

She had to think about it, for like two seconds. Her

shoulders slowly shrugged, answering him. She shook her head. "It hasn't really felt like home since I lost Blake. It's his furniture. I wanted something different, but he really loved this, so I was okay with it too." She spoke slowly. "The wall colors are his choices. I wanted bright and cheerful, but he wanted the browns and caramels."

"You could buy new furniture and repaint the walls, if that was the only issue."

She shook her head. "No, it was Blake who made this home. Without him, well ..." She shifted from Kanen's lap to sit beside him again, subconsciously separating herself from him.

He let her go, but he didn't completely release her.

She stared down at their fingers laced together. "I have some friends here but not good ones."

"And what about your friends in California? Do you still have them?"

"Well, there's you," she said with a bright smile. "And I never did thank you for coming to my rescue."

He shook his head and placed a finger against her lips. "No thanks needed," he whispered.

She kissed his finger and watched as his eyes deepened in color. "Are you sure we should walk down this path?" she asked hesitantly.

The corner of his mouth kicked up. "I don't see any reason why not. Do you?"

She didn't have any reason, except a part of her still held back because it felt wrong. "I just wonder if Blake will always be between us," she said hesitantly. "And moving to California seems like leaving him behind."

Understanding lit his gaze. He gathered her in his arms and cuddled her close. She didn't fight him, just lay against his chest.

"I wouldn't want him to be there, always between us, and I think, if we were to become more than friends, he would be," she finally whispered.

"Blake will be wherever we put Blake," Kanen said firmly. "He was a friend to both of us. He was your husband, but he was my best friend. And he's not here with us now. So I understand that he'll always be there in our memories, our thoughts, but I don't think he has to be *between* us. There's no reason he can't sit off to the side and be a part of our lives. We don't want to forget him. We don't want to avoid using his name. We want to remember the good times. Some of our memories are shared. Sometimes we had the same adventures with him. The last thing we want is to be worried about not bringing up his name in a conversation. If we try to avoid having him with us, that's what will happen. So I suggest we just let things develop naturally between us and don't worry about it if Blake memories arise."

She chuckled. "Is life so simple for you?"

He shrugged. "It makes it a little easier to get through everything in my world with the least amount of stress."

She thought about that and nodded. "Okay, just so you know, there will be times when I get worried about you and your career."

"Okay, just so you know, there'll be times when I may get worried about you too," he commented.

She frowned. "What would you be worried about?"

He smiled. "About the fact that you might always be comparing me to him."

"What?" She shook her head. "I'd never do that. You're so very different." She thought about it and realized, "It would be subconscious if I did."

"It would be natural if you did." His voice was full of acceptance.

She nodded in understanding. "You're both so very different, and I love you both," she said quietly. "It's hard to comprehend he's gone. But, after almost a year, I've finally come to terms with it—I think."

"Good," he said, giving her a big hug. "Because I like what you just said."

Startled, she looked up at him. And then realized she'd said she loved them both. She smiled. "You know I love you. I've told you often enough."

"But there's *love*, and then there is *in love*," he said. "I'm quite happy if you go from one to the other."

She shook her head. "Oh, no, no, no. Not unless you'll go there too."

"How do you know I'm not already there?" he asked with a chuckle. "There's a lot you don't know about me."

"And there's a lot you don't know about me." She smiled back at him.

"Well then, I suggest we keep the communication line open, and we get to know each other a little better, even though we think we've always known each other. This is the perfect time to see just what might be there."

"How are we supposed to get to know each other under these circumstances and with your two friends around?"

He smirked and said, "We'll find a way."

KANEN PICKED HER up in his arms and carried her into the kitchen. The men were there, waiting for them, big grins on their faces. With great ceremony, they pulled out a chair at the head of the table, let Kanen place her there, and Nelson said, "Madam, your meal is served."

She laughed out loud. "Hey, I don't know what to do with you guys spoiling me so much."

They shrugged, and Taylor said, "Sometimes you need that."

What followed was a meal anybody would have been proud of. Kanen's eyebrows rose as he saw pork chops grilled to perfection with an absolutely delicious-looking hollandaise sauce draped over the top, a sautéed vegetable mix he'd never seen before and even biscuits on the side.

Nelson said, "It's a bit of an eclectic mix, but we were working with what we had."

She held her hands together in delight. "I don't care what you call it or how eclectic this looks because it smells delicious. I had no idea this much food was in my apartment."

Just then Taylor returned to the table and placed a rice dish beside her. "This one needed an extra minute."

It was yellow and fragrant and had spices all over the top, plus dried herbs. She sniffed the air and said, "This is fantastic. You guys can cook for me anytime."

They chuckled as everyone sat down.

Kanen was about to take his seat, when his phone rang. The others looked at him. He stepped back out to the living room to answer. "Mason, what's up?"

"I just heard from MI6," he said. "I understand you had a crazy afternoon."

"We did," Kanen said, realizing he'd forgotten to update Mason. "Did they catch him?"

"No. They put out an all-points bulletin for Bob. His vehicle was found ditched on the side of the road, with no sign of the driver."

"Of course not," Kanen said with a groan. "Which means he could be anywhere. The women at his store were very loyal. They would easily have lent him their vehicles, if needed."

"The MI6 guys thought of that, and the employees' vehicles are being watched."

"Good," Kanen said.

"How is Laysa holding up?"

"Bob left her an *I'll be back* note in her apartment. First she was scared. Then she got mad. She recognized him in the store, even though he wore a balaclava while holding her. He has very distinctive wrists and forearms," Kanen said. "And that made a big difference to her. She could easily identify him and recognized his voice. Once he realized the gig was up, he bolted."

"Which always makes a guilty man look guiltier," Mason said with a chuckle.

"Exactly."

"Makes MI6 more cooperative too."

"We're just about to sit down to a hot meal. Then we'll get back to it."

"MI6 is tracking down everybody in the blackmail photos. They've identified and found the last two previously unknown men, both who admitted to being blackmailed but said the blackmail is of no value now because their circumstances have changed."

"So, if the photos are no longer of any value," Kanen said, "why the devil does Bob care?"

"We'll ask him when we find the man and hopefully get answers to end this mystery."

"True enough." Kanen pocketed the phone and went back into the kitchen, where everybody dug into the food. "I hope you left me some," he protested.

Laysa chuckled. "Those who come late to the dinner table will have whatever dregs are left," she misquoted with a grin.

He protested again loudly.

She quite happily handed him whatever was left on the platters. There wasn't much. Still, it was a full plate by the time he had dished up servings of everything. Then he told them what Mason had said.

The conversation dimmed from laughter to the looming specter over their world.

She nodded. "We need to figure out why he's doing this, and everything else will come together."

"Money, sex or power," Kanen said. "Those are generally the reasons we do things."

She stared at him. "Surely not. There has to be a lot of other reasons."

"You mean, like jealousy?" Nelson asked with a smirk. "That could go under sex or power."

Her face wrinkled up. "I don't think you guys have a very good attitude."

They chuckled.

"We do have a fairly balanced one," Kanen said. "The problem is, we've seen an awful lot that you haven't. You're just now being touched by it, realizing how absolutely twisted many people are. But, to the bad guys, their motives are always reasonable. To them anyway."

"So it's reasonable, to Bob, to hold me captive. To beat me up."

"If he needed those pictures and had left them with Blake, absolutely. He thinks it's the means to the end. That it's totally justified."

"At least he didn't kill me," she said. "So, from that perspective, the damage to me is minimal."

"True," Kanen said. *But for how long?*

They finished eating and were doing the dishes when a knock came at the door. Everyone froze. Kanen motioned Nelson to take her to another room, and Kanen stepped up to the door. There was no peephole, and he hated that. He opened the door to see a stranger. "Yes? May I help you?"

The man frowned. "Where is Laysa?"

From the bedroom Laysa called out, "Carl, I'm here."

Kanen recognized his name, the man who she'd stayed with that first night. Kanen motioned to the living room. "I'm a friend of hers. Come on in."

But Carl didn't appear to want to step inside. He looked at Kanen suspiciously. "When did you arrive?"

"A couple days ago," Kanen said. "Right after she contacted me, I came running. But then long-term friends are like that."

Carl looked at him and said, "How long have you been friends?"

"Long before Blake passed away," Kanen said.

Laysa suddenly appeared at Kanen's side. She smiled up at Carl. "Hey, how are you?"

He looked at her with relief on his face. "Are you okay? I came down yesterday, and, when you didn't answer, I got worried."

She reached out a hand and grasped his. "I'm sorry. I should have let you know we flew to Spain and back. I have been out with the guys quite a bit, trying to find my assailant. This is Kanen, the friend I told you about. He's been looking after me."

She turned to Kanen. "Carl is my neighbor and a policeman, who opened his home to me when I escaped and kept me safe until you arrived."

Kanen reached out a hand with a smile. "Thank you for watching over her. She went through a terrible ordeal."

Carl nodded and shook Kanen's hand but still looked suspiciously at Kanen. Carl motioned down the hallway for Laysa to come out there to talk to him. It was all Kanen could do not to yank her back to his side. He waited at the doorway with his head cocked, trying hard to hear their conversation. But he didn't hear much, just whispered voices.

Then she smiled at Carl and said, "It's all right. Everything's good." And she headed back toward Kanen. With her apartment door closed, she said, "Carl was afraid you looked a little too dangerous to be on my side. He wanted to make sure I was safe and not being held captive again."

Nelson snorted. "Yeah, that's our Kanen. Dangerous to look at."

"At least he had your well-being in mind," Kanen said. "He seems like he cares."

She nodded. "He's been a good neighbor. He lives just one floor above me."

As far as Kanen could tell, anybody close to Laysa deserved a second look. Just to make sure Carl really was a good guy and not involved in this mess. And that brought up something else Kanen should have considered. No one had ever questioned if Bob could be working with a partner. Kanen caught Taylor's eye, who appeared to be thinking the same thing.

Taylor walked back into the living room, sat down with his laptop and opened it up.

In a casual conversational tone, Kanen asked her, "How

long has Carl lived here?"

She shrugged. "I don't know. A few years before Blake and I moved here."

"What's his last name?"

That was one question too many. She planted her hands on her hips and glared at him. "There's nothing wrong with him. He's a good guy. A cop. You be nice."

He opened his eyes wide and gave her an innocent look. "Anyone connected to you is someone I will take a second look at," he said. "So I get that you don't want me prying into people's lives who may have nothing to do with this, but I won't know they have nothing to do with this until I pry."

He waited for her answer. He could see the younger version of the woman in front of him. As a child, she would have stomped her foot several times in frustration. Right now all she did was glare at him.

Then she turned to face Taylor, narrowed her gaze. "Are you in on this?"

He turned a bland face in her direction. "I don't know what you're talking about."

She raised both hands, palms up, in mock surrender. "Fine. Whatever. His name is Carl McMaster." She spun around and sat on the couch with more force than necessary. "His wife's name is Sicily. She's lovely too. They are good people."

The men busily tapped away on their keyboards.

Kanen sat beside her and said, "Remember that, whatever we do, we're doing for your sake."

She released a heavy sigh and nodded. "I get that. But it's still very intrusive. Not to mention the fact no one wants to contemplate that Carl could be involved."

"A lot of people could be involved on a peripheral level,"

Kanen said. "That's why we do these checks and balances." Once again Kanen's phone rang. It was Mark, the gym manager. Kanen answered it quietly, keeping an eye on her. He was a little worried about how this all affected her.

"Hey, should have called you earlier. We had a break-in last night."

"Oh?" Kanen straightened and stood, walking to the living room window. "What was taken?"

"Nothing was taken, but Blake's locker was broken into."

Half under his breath, he whispered, "Shit."

"Exactly. So I presume whatever you took out of that locker ..."

"I'll make the same assumption," Kanen said. "Do you have video feed from last night?"

"I do, but the guy wore a black mask and kept his face away from the camera."

"What about outside in the parking lot? Any idea what vehicle he was driving?"

"No, I don't. The camera angle stops at the front door."

"Have you called the cops?"

"Should I? Nothing else was damaged, and I don't really want the added aggravation. Once people see the cops hanging around, all hell breaks loose."

"How about a quiet pair of MI6 agents coming through, looking for fingerprints?"

"Good idea. The guy on tape didn't wear gloves. So, if there are fingerprints, they would be around the locker."

"I'll call you right back." Kanen hung up and called his MI6 contact. "There was a break-in at Gold's gym last night. Somebody breaking into Blake's locker, presumably to find the bag of blackmail photographs."

MI6 arranged for a small team to go in and to take fingerprints after-hours.

"I'll call Mark back and warn him. I'll tell him to make sure nobody else touches the locker."

"You do that," the MI6 contact said. "But chances are it's already too late."

"I know." Kanen hung up and redialed Mark. Once he explained about MI6, he said, "I know it's probably too much to ask, but, if you could make sure nobody touches the locker or the door frame, lock, etc., it would be appreciated."

Mark gave a half laugh. "As you saw, it's the last locker in a bank of lockers. I have no idea how many million fingerprints would be on it, especially since men often grab on to it as they swing around the corner."

"Understood." Kanen hung up, turned to look at the others and said, "Our photographer guy is getting closer. He broke into Blake's locker at the gym last night."

"He obviously had the same idea we did," Nelson said. "And maybe he even saw us go into the gym and had to check for himself."

"He'll either assume we have it or he will keep looking for it," Kanen said.

"We didn't check the storage unit though," Taylor reminded them.

"No," Laysa said, frowning at them. "I completely forgot about it."

The men checked their watches.

Kanen said, "I suggest we go now. We have several hours of daylight. Let's make good use of this time. Even though we think we have what this guy is looking for, maybe we can draw him out, see if we can set him up and take him down at the storage facility."

She brightened. "Particularly if he sees us leave here."

Kanen smiled. "Exactly." He met Nelson's gaze over her head and knew they were both thinking the same thing. There had to be some way to set a trap for this guy. But how?

CHAPTER 13

L AYSA LED THE way to the storage unit. They'd parked farther down on the street, so nobody would know easily where they went.

Kanen came up to her side, reached gently for her hand and whispered in your ear, "Give us the number. Let us take a look and make sure nobody's here or anywhere around."

She shot him a look, then shrugged. With Nelson once again standing at her side, Kanen and Taylor took off. She faced Nelson and asked, "How come you're on babysitting duty?"

"Because I love looking after babies," he said with a smirk.

She shot him a sideways look.

He grinned and said in a more gallant one, "It's an honor to look after the lady."

"Don't you miss out on the action?"

"I get plenty of action," he said.

Something in his tone made her think he was talking about a completely different kind of action. They waited on the spot in silence. She glanced around and realized Kanen had left her in a rather unique area, a path leading to the back of the storage units. They'd already gone through the gate, but they were surrounded by tall cedar trees and were out of everybody's view.

"It's really isolated here, isn't it?" she asked.

"It is. It's a great place for an ambush."

Instinctively she took a step closer to him.

He chuckled. "That works every time."

She smacked him lightly on the shoulder. "If that works with all the girls, you should be ashamed of yourself."

"Oh, I am. I am." He tried to sound serious.

She just rolled her eyes at him.

Suddenly Kanen stood in front of her, his gaze going from one to the other.

Was that worry in his eyes? "You okay?" she asked.

He looked at her in surprise. "I'm fine. The coast is clear."

He reached out a hand, and she placed hers in it. As they walked along together, she looked around to see that Nelson had disappeared. "What's going on?" she asked. "You show up, and now Nelson leaves. Like musical chairs. Plus, when you arrived, you looked worried."

"Of course I'm worried," he said. "What if you prefer Nelson to me?"

"As if," she snorted. "A new friend is always nice to have, but it certainly isn't a replacement for an old one."

"No, but a shiny new penny is always more attractive than the dull old one you've been carrying around."

She realized his tone held a note of insecurity. She squeezed his fingers and whispered, "I don't prefer him over you. I don't prefer either of them over you. Honestly, you're the best man I know."

He squeezed her fingers now, then stopped her as she started to go around the corner.

She hesitated, watching as he studied the surroundings, never losing that sharp attentive look as he searched through the buildings, almost as if he had X-ray vision, seeing what went on inside each one.

"Do you really think he'd come here?"

"I think he has no choice," Kanen said. "We're only here to check it out, to make sure nothing else is here that we should know about."

When he felt it was safe, he took a step forward, tugging her gently along behind him, always protecting her, always keeping his body between her and any assailant. She wondered at that. Was there ever a more certain man born with a protective gene? Was Kanen born with that instinctive need to look after others? She certainly hadn't been born with it. At that thought, she wondered what kind of a mother she'd make.

For a long time, that was all she'd thought about, but, since Blake had been so against having children, she had tried to not push it too hard.

Apparently she had, though. Blake had struggled with that. And that was sad. She hadn't wanted to bring him any heartache. Yes, she wanted a family. But she wondered if she could look after her child as well as Kanen looked after her.

Or maybe that was a genetic skill that blossomed when you got pregnant and had a child. She'd never even babysat when she was growing up. She was an only child and had basically been orphaned at a young age. Now she had to wonder about her mothering instincts. Did she have any?

Luckily those thoughts were interrupted as she neared her storage unit. She pulled her key ring from her pocket and found her spare key to open the lock on the door. This was a key lock, not a combination lock. She studied it for a long moment, trying to remember when they'd put it on. And why this kind of a lock versus the other? But she gave up.

She had no way to know what was in her husband's mind at the time.

As she stepped back with the lock in her hand, the men grabbed the handles on either side of the rolling garage door and slowly raised it. She hadn't been here in a long time and assumed nothing had changed. But, as they flicked on the lights, she realized everything had changed. "I don't know what all this stuff is," she said.

"What do you mean?" Nelson stepped forward, blocking her view. She was forced to look at him. "Are you saying this isn't your unit?"

She looked around him, returning her attention to the contents. "I don't know. It's my lock." She held up the key still in the lock in her hand. "But I don't remember the unit being this full." He stepped out of the way as she walked forward, looking at the furniture. "For all I know, Blake, being Blake, might have let somebody else put their stuff in here too."

"*Interesting*," Kanen said. "More questions we should have asked him before he died, huh?"

She didn't know what to say, but Kanen seemed to have second thoughts about Blake. She spun to look at Kanen. "But you know what Blake was like. If anybody needed anything ..."

Kanen nodded. "I do, indeed, know all about that. And it is definitely something he would do. If you only had a portion of this storage unit filled, he would easily help somebody out by offering them the free space."

"He had the unit before we got married. We stored some stuff in here, but it wasn't even close to full. You and I moved some stuff here after Blake passed away, ... but again it wasn't this full. Someone put more in here after Blake's death." Several narrow walkways seemed to be between items, as if people had been back and forth, among all this stuff. "The thing is, I'm the one with the lock and the key. So, unless somebody has duplicate keys ... Well, Bob did force me to give him my spare key, but I didn't give him the correct unit number." She studied the couch underneath a few boxes. "I don't even know whose couch that is," she said in confusion. "I've never seen it before."

She walked farther down this path and stopped in front of a filing cabinet that was easily accessible, enough room so that the drawers could open. She tried to open one, but it was locked. She glanced back at Kanen. "This isn't my filing cabinet. And it's locked."

He pulled a small tool kit from his back pocket. "It's your storage unit," he said, "so let's find out what's in here. Maybe it'll tell us whose stuff is stored here."

He quickly broke into the filing cabinet. She didn't even see how he'd done it, he was so fast. She studied the tool kit in his hand, then raised her gaze to his.

He gave her a crooked smile and said, "My SEALs training has offered many avenues for future career potential." He pulled open the top drawer, finding it full of files.

As she flipped through them, she gasped. "These are all photographs. *All* of these are photographs." But they weren't photographs of people in compromising positions, they were like portrait photos. As they checked the folders, names were on the top. "Are these proofs? So people can call and ask for more copies or something?"

"That's how it would have been done in the olden days," Kanen said, "but, with the digital photos now, it's obviously very different."

She nodded. "But this points to somebody hanging on

to all the old photos."

"True."

They went through drawer after drawer after drawer. "These literally are all from one business, Finest Photos," she said.

"And they're all old," Kanen confirmed. "If you look at the dates, they're all from before 1995, when the poor man was charged with blackmailing his clients and was sentenced to jail."

She spun around. "None of this makes any sense. Why is this Finest Photos stuff in my storage unit?"

"A question we'd like to ask you ourselves," said two men from the entrance.

She spun to see the same two MI6 officers who had been at the photographer's shop. She frowned at them. "Oh, did Kanen tell you we were coming here?"

"Yes, but we should have known about this unit earlier."

Unbelievably she looked at them. "This is a storage unit my husband and I have. But this isn't my stuff."

"Can you prove that?" the first man said, his voice soft.

Her blood froze. "You can't possibly think I'm involved in this."

Kanen pulled her closer. "Nobody thinks you're involved," he said in a hard voice, his gaze never leaving the two men in front of them. "The agents might try using the element of fear, to see if they can shake some answers out of you, but that obviously won't work now either. And it's certainly not a technique I approve of."

The two men stared back at him, their faces bland.

"Kanen?" she asked, her voice low. "What are they doing here?"

"We'll all find answers together. Unless," he firmly said

to the men, "you're planning on charging her with something right now."

The men measured each other, and then finally the MI6 agents shook their heads. "We came here for answers. We're not ready to charge anyone yet," the first man said, but he left that threat hanging in the air.

Kanen felt Laysa tremble in his arms. He held her tight and said, "It's all good. You've done nothing wrong."

"But what if Blake did?" she whispered in a voice so low and so full of pain that nobody could mistake how the thought hurt her.

"We're not going there until we have a real reason to," Kanen said. "Blake was my best friend too. If he was involved in something, we can't ask him questions because he's gone. We can only pick up the pieces of what he's left behind and hope we can sort it out properly."

The agents came forward. Even though it was cramped in the storage unit, they pulled open a drawer to the filing cabinet and took a look for themselves.

"Don't look at me," Laysa snapped at them. "I'm just as confused as you guys are."

Taylor, from the other side of the unit, said, "Let's all calm down and start analyzing what we've got here. Obviously somebody has used this place for a long time. But why and who? What's the chance Blake found the bag here and moved it to the gym locker?"

The color drained from her face. "In which case you're implying my husband *was* involved in some way."

He shook his head. "No, only that he found what he thought were incriminating photos and decided to pull them out of the equation. We don't know anything yet, but I suggest we take the opportunity to find out."

THE NEXT HOUR was spent sorting through as much of the storage unit as possible. There were boxes full of paperwork, which appeared to be all the leftover files, photos, prints and negatives from the grandfather's chain of stores that closed in 1995. It didn't help in finding the current owner of this collection, but it was fascinating reading.

One box she got excited about. "It's all the court documents," she said. "Look."

Kanen flipped through the files and realized they were transcripts of the court case, copies of legal documents filed on the man's behalf. "I'm sure it's fascinating reading," he said, "but I'm not sure how important it is to us now."

"But we know there's a connection," she said. "I just don't know what it is."

Out of the corner of his eye, Kanen caught a movement. He spun to look at the front entrance. Some of the sunlight was fading, but it was still light enough inside to see clearly.

Leaving her in the middle of all the men, Kanen stepped out to the open side of the storage unit and took a look around. A truck was parked near another unit. The truck bed was open, and people were moving furniture out of the unit into the back of the truck. Taking a chance, Kanen walked around the block of units. There were ten storage units in each of the blocks, five facing one way and another five backed up to the others, facing the other way.

He walked to his right through the back and around to the front, looking for a sign of anybody having been here. But he found no new footprints in the grass, and, from the front, the area appeared to be empty.

As he returned, one of the MI6 guys stepped forward and asked, "Did you see anything?"

Kanen shook his head. "I can't help feeling we're being watched anyway."

"That makes sense. We have two men on watch."

While Kanen felt much better hearing that, he didn't like anything else about this. Bob was desperate to get whatever it was he wanted. As far as Kanen was concerned, it was the photos from the gym locker. What he wanted to know was how did the guy know the images had been here? Was it just a lucky guess? Maybe he'd seen them here?

Or ... did this come full circle back to the gym manager—Mark?

Kanen pulled out his phone, and, as the MI6 guys worked beside him, he called Mark. "So who did you tell?" he asked without preamble.

Silence loomed for a long moment. "What are you talking about?"

"You heard me. Who did you tell that we'd been to see Blake's gym locker?"

CHAPTER 14

S HE HEARD KANEN'S voice somewhere in the vicinity of the storage unit's opening, but she was kind of stuck in the back, busy looking in boxes of paperwork. It was fascinating to think that the entire photography shop business had ended up here. But also made her think Bob had to have been the one to store this here. Who else would have all this material? But none of that explained how this stuff ended up in *her* storage unit.

With all these thoughts rolling through her head, she wasn't sure what to think. She looked up, peered around the boxes but saw no sign of Kanen. She turned to Taylor and Nelson and asked, "Where did he go?"

Neither man looked up. "He's doing a perimeter walk," one said. "Nothing to worry about," the other one added.

"Are you sure about that?" she asked. The back of her neck twinged; she didn't feel anywhere near as confident as they seemed to be.

Nelson looked up and studied her. "What's the matter?"

"I think something is wrong." She snapped closed the file in her hand and stormed toward the front of the storage unit. There she looked around but still found no sign of Kanen.

Both Taylor and Nelson joined her. They stopped her from walking outside near the main roadway. "You're not going after him," Nelson said, his voice hard. "Let me contact him, and we'll see what's up."

She waited anxiously, her nerves getting the better of her as she waited for Nelson to text Kanen. The problem was, if he was in trouble, he needed to stay hidden, and the *ping* of texts would give him away. A phone call could be much worse. If Kanen didn't have his cell on Silent mode, it could put him in a lot of danger.

When there was no answer, Nelson and Taylor exchanged hard glances. They marched her back to the MI6 men. Taylor said, "She stays with you. We'll look for our friend."

Instantly the suited men were on alert. "What's happened?"

"Kanen has disappeared and isn't answering his phone," Taylor said.

The men pulled weapons, tucked her behind them and motioned for Taylor and Nelson to go.

She could hardly breathe now. She kept thinking about all the things that could have gone wrong with Kanen. But the agents weren't interested in listening to her attempts to get them all to go after her friends.

The agents stared at her, their faces bland and hard.

"And what if the other two are walking into a trap?"

"Then they're walking into a trap," one agent said.

She wanted to call them Cheech and Chong, just so she had a way to tell him apart. Both men were about five foot, ten inches tall. Both had dark brown hair. Both were long and lean and had a mean look on their faces when they wanted to. Most of the time, they looked like ordinary men. Maybe that was part of the magic of MI6 agents, that they had the ability to be completely unassuming and to blend into a crowd without any discernible, memorable features.

As it was, she wasn't in any way happy to be left behind. She pretended to go back to looking through the files. And then she smelled something at the rear of the storage unit. She turned and yelled, "Smoke!"

It came from a small hole underneath the storage unit. Suddenly flames shot through the hole.

She watched as the boxes of paperwork caught fire. The men hustled her forward to the front of the unit. She looked at them and said, "You do realize what they're trying to do, right?"

They didn't say a word, just shunted her between them and rushed her in between the two blocks of storage units. All of them were accessible from the outside. She presumed these units backed up into other units.

She turned to look at the agents. "Somebody started the fire in the unit behind this one. Go check it out!"

They just crossed their arms over their chests. She glared at them. "Then I will." She dashed forward. One of the agents tried to grab her and missed. She picked up speed, raced around the corner, counting off the same number of units until she came to the one that backed up to hers.

The door was down. A lock hung on the outside. Swearing to herself, knowing the agents were right on her heels, she went to lift the lock—finding it just resting there, not clicked together—when a bullet pinged into the door above her head. Now she was really in trouble. Someone outside was shooting at her.

She flattened to the ground, noting the fading sunlight. She decided to quickly stand and pop the lock, dropping again to push up the big rolling garage door, enough that she'd get in this adjoining storage unit by crawling underneath the door. She was a sitting duck in the unit, but at least the door was between her and the bullets.

Inside, with the storage unit door about six inches up off the floor, she turned on the light and stared. Wisps of smoke trickled along the back wall, shared by this unit and hers. This unit was almost completely empty, except for a desk that had been set up like an office. As she inspected the bulletin boards around the desk, she realized this was more of a central station, a control room, so to speak. Whoever was doing this had used this particular storage unit as his base for whatever his plans were. How strange. But it also meant he knew she was in here, and, with the light on, she was beyond just a sitting duck. If he didn't get to her, the smoke would soon enough.

She quickly moved to the desk to see if there was anything of interest. There were pictures of gyms. Pictures of weightlifters. Even a picture of her beloved husband.

She reached out with two fingers and stroked his face. It had to have been taken close to a year ago, just before he died. He'd had a mustache then. It had been a relatively new look for him, and this picture showed him with one. She didn't understand why Bob, the photographer, her assailant, had these gym photos. *Unless Bob really had met my husband at the gym?*

Just when she thought she might have a chance to figure it out, the big door behind her shifted. The light went out. She swore and squatted, hiding underneath the desk, the only item in the whole unit.

Bob said, in a mocking voice, "You really expect to hide here? You think I don't know where you are?"

She groaned. "It's you! How the hell did you know my storage unit was on the other side of this one?"

"That's easy," he said. "It used to be my unit. The reason your husband ended up with it was because I told him that I had some space, and I let him use it."

"You let him use it?" She was distracted momentarily by the increased smoke gathered around her on the floor at the back of this unit. *This is not good.*

"Basically I subleased it to him. And then asked him if he minded me adding some material to it. He said he didn't care. But ... *then* he did care. However, after he was dead, it didn't matter because you didn't seem to even know the storage unit was here. And I wanted the space, so I moved all my shit back over there again. I would get rid of your stuff eventually, but there didn't seem to be any point since you never came here. It was just more work, and I didn't need more of that."

In the darkness she could hear the same raspy voice of the man who had beaten her. "Did you find what you were looking for, Bob?" She stifled back a cough, refusing to appear even more helpless to this asshole.

"No," he snapped. "And, for that, I blame you and those asshole men you hooked up with. Blake would have given it back to me. And, if he hadn't died, we wouldn't be having this problem."

"If he hadn't died, *I* wouldn't be having a lot of problems," she cried out with anguish in her voice. "Do you even hear what you just said?" Then she let her voice drop in volume as she stared into the darkness in the direction he'd spoken from, her eyes now stinging from the smoke. "Did you kill him?" She hated to bring it up, but she had to know.

"Hell no. That wouldn't have served me well, would it?"

She closed her eyes, her shoulders sagging in relief. "Oh, thank God."

"I wondered if he didn't commit suicide though," Bob said, his voice thoughtful. "He sure bitched enough."

She didn't want Bob to continue. She didn't want Bob to break the lovely memories she held of her husband and their relationship. But it was like the asshole knew it was her weakness.

"Blake kept complaining about how you wanted a family, and he wanted nothing to do with that. But you wouldn't stop nagging him."

Each word was like a little stab wound to her heart. Had she really been so hard on Blake? It had been important to her, but they could have talked more. He could have told her how much it bothered him. Why hadn't he? She can't read minds.

"You know he was planning on leaving you, right?"

She sucked in her breath.

"I guess not. At least not from your shocked reaction. He really liked a woman at the gym. I figured he might go for it. But, even then, he seemed to pull back. Torn between two options. That's one of the reasons why I wondered if he'd chosen suicide as an easy out. Couldn't stand the idea that he'd break your heart or something foolish like that. But obviously he wasn't happy. He needed to get out from under you."

She swallowed hard several times, hating what he was implying. "I don't believe you," she whispered, unable to control her coughing now.

"I don't give a shit if you believe me or not," he said, coughing too. "I still want those photographs."

She closed her eyes, realizing the pictures were what he wanted. "MI6 has them all," she said wearily. "What difference do the photos make? They're old pictures. All the blackmails have been paid, and the victims don't give a shit anymore. Some of them are even dead."

"I know," he said, coughing more. "I've always known that."

She shook her head. "So why do you care now? What difference does any of it make?"

"Because my great-uncle was the blackmailer. And my grandfather paid the price," he said in a conversational tone. "My great-uncle is a very wealthy man now. He's insisting I don't get any of it. I want those photos to go with the other information I have, which proved he was the blackmailer. Because, if nothing else, I'll see his carcass rot in jail for the last years of his life. But, before then, I'll blackmail him for all the goddamn money he stole from all these people, ruining my grandfather's life as well as mine."

"Did you kill him?"

"Hell no," he said, "But I can thank my great-uncle for that too."

"Your great-uncle has to be quite old by now."

"Not as old as you might think," he said. "My grandfather was the oldest, and my great-uncle was a step sibling from yet another marriage. He was a good twenty-plus years younger than my grandfather. He was almost the same age as my father. And, for that reason alone, I thought my father should have done something to fix the problem, but he was too weak. Either too weak or too easily swayed by my great-uncle. Not that he and Grandfather ever got along very well, but Grandfather was a great man. He built a huge business across Europe. He was well-known for his work. And my great-uncle ruined him, ruined his name, ruined our family name and took away the legacy that was mine by rights."

The sordid tale of betrayal and murder was something

that could be told and retold at any street corner around the world. Was there anything more vindictive and hateful than a family member consumed by jealousy or greed?

"I'm sorry," she whispered, coughing more often now. "I'm sorry for your grandfather. That must have been extremely hard on him."

"You have no idea," the younger man in front of her said.

"So why did you wait all this time? You had the photos."

"Because he has yet another wife, and this time there's a child," he said, his voice turning vindictive. "And my great-uncle made it very clear that I would get nothing. He stole everything from our family, and now he'll give it to that baby who knows nothing of his ill-gotten inheritance."

"And now ... you think these photos ... will make a difference?" she asked, among coughs, not quite understanding. She could certainly understand the trigger when the great-uncle had a family to hand down the fortune to. "Did he tell you ... beforehand ... it was all yours?"

"He promised it was all mine, if I kept my mouth shut," he said, his words interrupted by coughs. "Because he was already ill, I didn't think anything of it. ... For the last few years, I took whatever he would give me, ... just small sums to tide me over, but he wouldn't give me ... very much. Or enough to live on." Bob was overtaken by a spate of coughing, then resumed his explanation. "Despite his illness, he got a young woman pregnant. ... Supposedly pregnant. ... The first thing I wanted to do was test for DNA, but he wouldn't let me. ... He's tickled pink at the idea of finally having a son. And ... he also made it very clear that, ... if I did anything to disrupt his family, I'd get nothing."

"So don't disrupt his family, and you still get everything," she said, finding it harder to breathe, to keep her wits about her. Surely it was worse for Bob, right? Didn't smoke rise? Aren't we told to drop and roll?

"Are you a fool?" More coughing ensued. "No way he'll give me anything." Bob drew a labored breath.

She could hear him moving about, probably moving closer to the opening, hoping for less smoke there.

"He now has a son of his own. ... The last thing he wants is to give anything to my family."

"But they're just old photos," she said. "None of it is enough to prove anything."

"Except that I have the bookkeeping ledgers that relate to the men in the photos. And that's the proof I need to confirm the blackmail payments. Because I also have the case files from my grandfather's court case. ... And, because he was murdered, this is the motive for his death. I get revenge on my grandfather's murder. I'll blackmail my uncle so he turns the money over to me, and I get to watch him suffer through his last few years, poor and broke, like my grandfather suffered. ... If my great-uncle won't cooperate, then I'll turn over everything to the cops, and they can prosecute the real blackmailer and murderer." Bob chuckled. "Regardless, if my great-uncle cooperates or not, I'll turn him over to the cops anyway."

"What about giving the money back to all those families he blackmailed?"

"That's their problem. They're the ones caught being fools," he snapped. "They've already lost the money. They paid it for silence, to wash away their sins." Bob let out a cackling laugh, ending in more coughs. "I won't be the same fool."

"So why did you give those pictures to Blake to hold?"

"Because he bragged about having the safest holding spot ever. That nobody would ever find his new hiding spot."

Laysa frowned. "Blake?"

"Yeah. I already knew about his gym locker. But, if he had a safe somewhere, I figured that would be one of the best places to hide everything."

"That makes no sense," she said. "Absolutely none."

He sighed. "No, you're right. It doesn't. That's because I'm lying. I was hoping to keep the last vestige of your beloved husband alive." His tone held heavy mockery. "Blake saw everything I had when I moved it all into the storage unit. He went through it and found the bag with all the photos. He stole it. ... It's how he would finance his exit from your marriage. He wanted money for it all. He knew how much it meant when he saw my reaction. ... He showed me the damn bag, then said he had the safest hiding place in the world. At the time I pretended indifference, and I walked. ... But I didn't walk far. I was trying to figure out what to do. So I tracked him. No, I didn't kill him. He truly died in an accident."

At this point the blows were coming too hard and too fast. She sat here stunned, completely overwhelmed by what Bob said. "I don't believe you," she cried out, tears washing the smoke out of her eyes and prodded along by the emotional pain Bob had inflicted.

"I don't give a damn if you believe me or not," he said, then seemed to fall to the ground or dropped to his knees.

Was he seeking oxygen? Was he overcome with the smoke?

"I've been working on this project for a long time. If my great-uncle hadn't produced an heir, I probably wouldn't have given a damn, thinking the money was coming my way.

But, after I talked to him and realized how things had changed, I couldn't let it go. ... And I wanted the photos back from your bloody husband. Once he realized they had value, he wanted money. But I didn't have any. So I waited, biding my time. ... Until the fool got himself killed. Then I went after you. I'd checked the storage unit but gave up. Then you made me think to look again. More time wasted as I couldn't find them here."

She bowed her head, wondering about the things he said. *Could they be true?* She really desperately wanted them not to be true. But how was she supposed to determine the truth? "And what now?" But he didn't answer. "I've told you that MI6 has the photos. When you go back to your great-uncle, just tell him you have proof—you still have the ledgers—and that he's to hand over all the money regard-less."

"No," he said, scrambling to stand it seemed. "He'd just tell the cops that I forged the ledgers. No, I need those photos. I want to see the look on his face when he realizes I've got them."

"Or maybe just hand over the ledgers and the rest of what you've got to MI6, and they can turn it all over to whatever jurisdiction needs to try your great-uncle."

"Either way, I need those photos."

Frustrated, she raised both palms. "Then talk to MI6. How many times do I have to tell you that?" By now she was choking from the smoke from the other side. "What if the photos were in there? In my side of the storage unit?" she asked. "Everything else, the court case files are in that unit too that you just burned up, not to mention all my own personal belongings."

"If you cared anything about Blake, you would have

come by sometime in the last twelve months," he said. "Believe me. Everything important to me in that storage unit is digitized—the ledger, the courtroom documents. I did that once I realized your lovely husband stole the original blackmail photos."

"You mean, you didn't digitize them earlier?"

He waved a hand. "No. Do you have any idea how many hours it took? But it's done now," he said wearily. "All except for those damn photos."

She started to cough heavier now. People banged on the outside of the large door to this unit. She screamed out for help, using up what little oxygen she had. She could hear people pounding, trying to open the door. She looked at Bob and said, "You've locked it, haven't you?"

"Yes," he said. "I figured, if you die without telling me where the photos are, those men will just throw me in jail. Then I really don't give a shit. Maybe I can sneak out with the smoke, when they open up the door to this unit. I don't know at the moment. I'm not sure I give a damn."

"What about all that vengeance?" she asked. "What about all the revenge in your heart? You wanted to get back at him, at your great-uncle."

Now Bob coughed too.

"What about just surviving for yourself?" she asked in desperation. "If you didn't kill anyone, you don't have much you can be charged with. Yes, you held me captive in my own home and beat me up. But that's what, a year, two years maybe? Probably just a slap on the wrist and probation." Her voice was bitter, knowing the judicial system and how fruitless it was if he was a first-time offender at least in the US but she had no clue here.

He started to speak and then bent over double, hacking

and coughing heavily.

She crawled to the big door, trying to lift it. There was just half an inch of space underneath the door. She lay closer to it on the floor, sucking in fresh air. "I'm in here," she cried out. "I'm in here."

She could hear the men doing something on the other side, but she wasn't sure they'd get to her in time. Smoke inhalation was ugly, and even now flames licked at the back of this unit. Not that much was here to burn, but there was a little. And the flames sucked up every bit of oxygen she had available.

She gazed at her captor, now rolling on the ground coughing, holding his chest. In the din she could hear Kanen calling to her, "Hang on. We're getting there."

Suddenly a knife cut the rubber edging right in front of her face, giving her a couple more inches of space for oxygen. She breathed in deep. She couldn't see him but for one eye, and he was right there, smiling at her.

"We're getting there, sweetheart. We're getting there."

And suddenly a heavy groaning and creaking came as the door broke free and rose. He reached for her, pulling her to him. She had one last heavy coughing spell and collapsed in his arms.

KANEN HAD NEVER been so damn scared in his life. When that garage door finally lifted, and all the smoke poured out, he thought for sure she was a goner. She collapsed in his arms, and he started CPR to clean out her lungs. He knew the medics were on the way, and the men collected around Kanen. They already had collared the asshole, Bob. But he'd passed out from the smoke too.

As he was loaded, handcuffed, into an ambulance, Kanen stood to the side and made sure he was secured and transported out of there. He also didn't want Laysa in the same ambulance with her captor, just in case. Thankfully a second ambulance showed up at the same time.

He rode alongside her as the paramedics worked on her. He could do nothing but hold her hand, urging her to keep fighting.

His mind was completely overwhelmed with everything he and the other men had heard. Although the big door had been down, it hadn't been soundproofed, so Bob's and Laysa's voices had easily carried outside. It was just stunning what this was all about. Revenge, greed, hatred.

If Bob was correct, his grandfather had served time for a crime he didn't commit and had been murdered by the same person who'd done the crime, Bob's great-uncle. Kanen knew the cops and MI6 would be all over this one, and he hoped they caught the asshole great-uncle. But he didn't think this Bob guy deserved to get any of the money. Not one dime. Not after what he'd done to Laysa.

Finally she was removed from the ambulance into the emergency area of the hospital, and thereafter, with tubes and an oxygen mask, she was tucked into a bed, stable but still not out of the woods. He sat in a chair beside her, holding her hand, kissing her fingers every once in a while and bowing his head to rest his forehead against the back of her hand as he whispered, "Come on, Laysa. Fight."

Finally she squeezed his hand, and he bolted to his feet. She tried to speak and started coughing. A nurse came in and removed the oxygen tube under her nostrils, pouring water into a cup and leaving it nearby.

"Call me if needed," the ER nurse said, leaving them

alone again.

Once the coughing cleared, Laysa had a sip of water and collapsed against the pillow, the bed at an angle so she could breathe easier. She smiled up at him. "Thanks for saving my life."

He shook his head, leaned down and kissed her hard. "Now that I've saved it, it's mine," he said. "Enough of this. You're coming back to California with me. You're moving into my apartment. Hopefully into my bed. And we'll have as many years as we can together. And, if life is good to us, we'll start a big family and live happily ever after. Blake's death highlights that obviously there is no guarantee we'll grow old on rocking chairs side by side, but, if I could ask for just one thing, it would be for that. I want to keep you safe and at my side forever." He was as serious as he could be. He watched tears come to the corner of her eyes and wiped them away. "Sweetheart, don't cry," he whispered. "Please don't cry."

She smiled and reached up, her hand covering his against her cheek, and she whispered, "That's what I would wish for too. Just keep me close." She closed her eyes and rested. Then her eyes popped open. "Get me the hell out of here so we can share a bed tonight. You can just hold me in your arms. I doubt I'm up for much more." She coughed again. "But it would be nice to not be in a hospital, not having anybody chasing after us, just for it to be the two of us. Just hold me please."

He snagged her into his arms, settled himself on the hospital bed and whispered, "As soon as you're discharged, we're getting out of here."

She rested her head on his chest and fell asleep.

CHAPTER 15

W HEN SHE WOKE the next time, she was being moved into a wheelchair. She stared up at Kanen. "Do I get to leave already?"

He nodded. "We're breaking you out," he said in a whisper. But his big grin belied his words. "Charles arranged it."

She smiled and said, "Ah, the secret, shadowy Charles. Will I ever meet him? Not right now though. I'm still so damn tired."

"And your chest will hurt for a long time," Nelson said. "There can be no exertion. Wheelchair all the way."

She wrinkled her nose up at him. "I'd rather not."

"Just to the cab," Kanen said. "I promise. And, before we head stateside, we'll stop in and meet the elusive but very excellent Charles."

He bundled her up in a blanket, and the cabbie drove them back to her place, where Kanen carried her to the elevator and up to her apartment.

She looked at him. "I knew you were strong but …"

"Sweetie, no way you're walking. No way I'm letting you out of my sight. Besides, right now, all I want to do is hold you." He carried her into the apartment and all the way to the bathroom, dropped her gently on her feet, and said, "Get ready for bed and then straight under the covers."

She coughed and nodded. "I can handle that."

Her nightgown hung on the back of the door. She changed into it, and, when she opened the door, her face scrubbed, her teeth brushed, he was right there to assist her across the room.

"I can walk, you know," she said and then started coughing. "You don't have to keep looking after me."

"How about we forget the looking after part, and stick with the keep part." He said flashing her a big grin. "I'll just *keep* you period." He kissed her gently then helped her into bed. "I'll get you a cup of tea. I'll be right back."

She nodded. "Fine."

By the time he returned, she was nodding off. She opened her arms. "Can you lie down with me?"

He chuckled. "I'm getting into bed with you." He closed the bedroom door, stripped down as he walked to the bed and crawled into it beside her. He wrapped her into his arms and drew her close. "Now sleep."

She smiled and murmured, "Thank you," and closed her eyes again.

But her dreams were full of bad guys and fire and smoke and chasing after Kanen because he had disappeared. She woke up, remembering. "Where were you?" she cried out, sitting up slightly.

He woke from his sleep and stared at her. "Did you have a bad dream?"

"The only reason I left the storage unit was because you were gone for longer than you should have been. You didn't answer your phone either. Do you know how terrified I was?"

"We were searching for Bob. And I couldn't answer my phone or the backlight would give away my position. When

I got back to the storage unit, it was engulfed in flames. I thought for sure you were still in there," he said.

She smiled at him. "Oh." She collapsed beside him again. "That makes sense." She leaned up on one elbow and kissed him. And then kissed him again and kissed him again. "You taste smoky," she said.

"No, I think it's you who tastes smoky," he said with a chuckle. He rolled her over gently onto her back. "You should be sleeping. You're still keyed up and sore from the CPR. It's too early for you to be awake."

"I'm fine," she announced, rolling over atop him again. "Besides, this is my bed, and you're in it. And I've thought about this a lot over the last few days. I'm really not prepared to let you leave until I'm ready."

His eyes lit with interest. "Oh? What did you have in mind?" His hands already tugged her nightgown, taking it over her hips, up to her ribs.

She could feel his bare skin beneath her, and a very interesting ridge nestled against her hips. She wiggled ever-so-slightly, watching his eyes turn a smoky color, and she chuckled. "I'm up for anything. Maybe a little gentle to begin with, but, after that, I suggest we see what might appeal."

One eyebrow rose. "Sweetheart, I'm up for anything anytime you are." And he bumped his hips up against her, so she could feel exactly what was up.

She chuckled, leaned over and kissed him gently. "Maybe you should prove that to me. I'm not exactly sure how this will work."

"I'm sure you understand how all of it works," he murmured teasingly.

His tongue traced the shape of her ear, sending shivers

down her back, his warm breath against her throat sliding down to warm the space between her breasts. When he cupped her plump round breasts, she moaned gently. She arched, filling his hands fully as she whispered, "But I've never done this with you, so maybe you're full of tricks I don't know anything about."

"No tricks," he murmured, "just love. Maybe now it's our time."

She sighed as he took one nipple into his mouth and suckled deeply. Feeling an answering tug deep in her groin, her belly tightened, and her body softened. She stroked his arms, sliding her fingers through his hair, kissing where she could reach.

As he shifted them both on their sides, facing each other, he gently and carefully treated her like a china doll as he explored her from one end to the other. By the time he slid his fingers along her leg, tickling the back of her knee, then to the inside of her thigh before finding the curls at the apex, she was already moist, ready and more than willing to take the next step.

As a matter of fact, she was past willing. She slid into demanding. She tugged on his arms, "Come to me," she ordered. "Now."

He chuckled. "So impatient," he murmured.

"Absolutely," she said. "I hate being thwarted when it's something I want." She grabbed his hair and tugged him gently toward her.

He rolled her to her back again, separating her legs wider as he hooked his arms under both her knees, and sat up, whispering, "Are you ready?"

Open, vulnerable and never more in love than she was right in that moment, she whispered, "Absolutely."

And he slid home. All the way to the heart of her. She cried out, her body tensing against a long year without any form of intimacy. He gave her a moment to relax, releasing her legs, his hands gently stroking her thighs and hips before cupping her breasts. Then he started to move.

She gave a cry of joy, her hips rising and falling, meeting him, matching him stride for stride, loving the feeling as the two came together, in a way of celebration, in a way of joy.

When he finally neared his release, she moved with him, harder and faster, a cry of urgency inside. She was so damn close.

Then he reached down between them, found that little nub between the folds of her skin, and her body exploded with her own climax, then his.

She lay shuddering in his arms, their bodies slick with sweat. She whispered, "That was a long time coming."

He rolled over, brushing her hair off her face and whispered, "No ghost?"

She knew what he was referring to. At some time she'd tell Kanen what her captor had said about Blake. She wanted to believe it was all lies, but she knew, no matter what was the truth, Blake was a part of her. And Kanen? ... Well, Kanen was a part of her too. Hopefully a permanent part of her future. She kissed him gently on his lips and whispered, "No ghost. Only angels singing. Because you gave me a touch of heaven. And it's a place I want to stay."

"With you in my arms," he whispered, "we're both in heaven, now and forever."

EPILOGUE

N ELSON BROWN SAT on the living room couch the next
morning. He folded up the blanket and set the pillow
on top. They were heading back today. He wasn't exactly
sure what Kanen and Laysa were planning on doing, but
Nelson figured it would take a few days to get her moved
over.

Everything in the storage unit that she'd owned with her
husband was lost. However, she still had an apartment full of
furniture to be dealt with. Taylor was making coffee. They'd
already booked flights for eleven o'clock this morning. They
were heading back to their regular jobs. First they were
scheduled to go for training—training they were anxious to
get to as it was on torpedoes. It was more of an information
session, but it was fascinating. Nelson wanted to see how the
bombs themselves were made. There was a lot of science and
engineering that went into them.

Taylor came toward him, holding up his phone. "Hey,
apparently there's officer training at the same time."

Nelson wrinkled his face. "Great. That may not be fun."

"A couple engineers are coming as well. They'll be on
staff, working on the deployment of the new torpedoes.
They're integrating a new chute system into the battleships."

Nelson nodded. "That part at least makes sense."

"Yeah. Remember the woman who gave that lecture we

went to? She talked about how the maintenance was so important on these chutes, and you got really mad at her because you felt she was implying the navy wasn't doing their job."

Nelson frowned. "Sort of. She was kind of arrogant."

Taylor nodded. "She was, indeed. But she's also the one who'll be part of this torpedo tour."

"Where's the tour?"

"On the USS *Independence*," Taylor said. "It would be good to go to the manufacturing plant, but that's not happening. At least we'll see them on the ship. She'll be there to show us how these are different from the older ones."

Nelson shrugged. "What difference does it make? They'll still have a certain payload. They'll still have an automatic delivery system. I doubt we'll have to retrofit anything on the battleships."

"Apparently something is different about these." He smiled. "She's not the speaker, but she's one of the engineers working on the project, so she'll be there."

"It doesn't matter to me," Nelson said. "I barely know the woman."

"That's good, but apparently she knows you."

Nelson looked up at Taylor and frowned. "What are you talking about?"

"I just got a text from Mason. Let me read it to you." He flicked through the texts on his phone, stopped and said, "*Make sure Nelson comes back with you. The engineer wants to speak with him specifically before the tour starts.*" Taylor looked at Nelson. "Does that mean anything to you?"

Nelson shook his head. "No. I don't know the woman. What the hell does she want with me?" Just then his phone buzzed. He saw a text from Mason.

Meeting one hour in advance of tour tomorrow morning, 8:00 a.m. on shore. At the dock.

He texted back with **What's this all about?**

Engineer wants to talk to you.

About what? he asked.

Mason typed **No clue. But she mentioned you specifically.**

I don't even know the woman.

Maybe but she knows you. Be there at 8:00 a.m. sharp.

Nelson tossed his phone on the coffee table, then snorted. "Who the hell is this woman? And why the hell does she give a damn about me?"

Taylor walked toward his buddy with two cups of coffee. "I guess you'll find out tomorrow morning, won't you?"

Nelson just stared at him. "Maybe. If I show up."

But it was only bravado. When the navy called, he stepped up each and every time. But it sure didn't stop him from wondering who this woman was and what she wanted with him.

This concludes Book 20 of SEALs of Honor: Kanen.

Read about Nelson: SEALs of Honor, Book 21

SEALS OF HONOR: NELSON
BOOK 21

Nothing is what it seems ... ever ...

Nelson's early morning meeting at the docks with Elizabeth Etchings offers only bad news. Her brother—and Nelson's old friend—has gone missing on his days off while his ship was docked in Ensenada. A trip to where he'd last been seen shows the local color ... and reveals Nelson's friend has gotten into bigger trouble than anyone could imagine.

Elizabeth might have had a hand in now sending two men to Baja to look for her brother, but she will not stay behind. Her brother is in danger ... and he's the only family she has left.

It doesn't take long for Nelson to realize that Elizabeth has caught the eye of someone who rules that corner of the world. She's now in jeopardy too—possibly more than her brother. Keeping her safe moves up Nelson's priority list.

Until both issues merge, and everything goes south ...

Book 21 is available now!

To find out more visit Dale Mayer's website.

http://smarturl.it/DMNelsonUniversal

Author's Note

Thank you for reading Kanen: SEALs of Honor, Book 20! If you enjoyed the book, please take a moment and leave a short review.

Dear reader,

I love to hear from readers, and you can contact me at my website: www.dalemayer.com or at my Facebook author page. To be informed of new releases and special offers, sign up for my newsletter or follow me on BookBub. And if you are interested in joining Dale Mayer's Reader Group, here is the Facebook sign up page. facebook.com/groups/402384989872660

Cheers,
Dale Mayer

COMPLIMENTARY DOWNLOAD

DOWNLOAD a *complimentary* copy of TUESDAY'S CHILD? Just tell me where to send it!

http://dalemayer.com/starterlibrarytc/

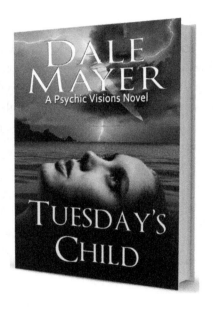

About the Author

Dale Mayer is a USA Today bestselling author best known for her Psychic Visions and Family Blood Ties series. Her contemporary romances are raw and full of passion and emotion (Second Chances, SKIN), her thrillers will keep you guessing (By Death series), and her romantic comedies will keep you giggling (It's a Dog's Life and Charmin Marvin Romantic Comedy series).

She honors the stories that come to her – and some of them are crazy and break all the rules and cross multiple genres!

To go with her fiction, she also writes nonfiction in many different fields with books available on resume writing, companion gardening and the US mortgage system. She has recently published her Career Essentials Series. All her books are available in print and ebook format.

Connect with Dale Mayer Online

Dale's Website – www.dalemayer.com
Twitter – @DaleMayer
Facebook – dalemayer.com/fb
BookBub – bookbub.com/authors/dale-mayer

Also by Dale Mayer

Published Adult Books:

Lovely Lethal Gardens
Arsenic in the Azaleas, Book 1
Bones in the Begonias, Book 2
Corpse in the Carnations, Book 3
Daggers in the Dahlias, Book 4
Evidence in the Echinacea, Book 5
Footprints in the Ferns, Book 6

Psychic Vision Series
Tuesday's Child
Hide 'n Go Seek
Maddy's Floor
Garden of Sorrow
Knock Knock...
Rare Find
Eyes to the Soul
Now You See Her
Shattered
Into the Abyss
Seeds of Malice
Eye of the Falcon
Itsy-Bitsy Spider
Unmasked
Deep Beneath

Psychic Visions Books 1–3
Psychic Visions Books 4–6
Psychic Visions Books 7–9

By Death Series
Touched by Death
Haunted by Death
Chilled by Death
By Death Books 1–3

Broken Protocols – Romantic Comedy Series
Cat's Meow
Cat's Pajamas
Cat's Cradle
Cat's Claus
Broken Protocols 1-4

Broken and... Mending
Skin
Scars
Scales (of Justice)
Broken but... Mending 1-3

Glory
Genesis
Tori
Celeste
Glory Trilogy

Biker Blues
Morgan: Biker Blues, Volume 1
Cash: Biker Blues, Volume 2

SEALs of Honor

Mason: SEALs of Honor, Book 1

Hawk: SEALs of Honor, Book 2

Dane: SEALs of Honor, Book 3

Swede: SEALs of Honor, Book 4

Shadow: SEALs of Honor, Book 5

Cooper: SEALs of Honor, Book 6

Markus: SEALs of Honor, Book 7

Evan: SEALs of Honor, Book 8

Mason's Wish: SEALs of Honor, Book 9

Chase: SEALs of Honor, Book 10

Brett: SEALs of Honor, Book 11

Devlin: SEALs of Honor, Book 12

Easton: SEALs of Honor, Book 13

Ryder: SEALs of Honor, Book 14

Macklin: SEALs of Honor, Book 15

Corey: SEALs of Honor, Book 16

Warrick: SEALs of Honor, Book 17

Tanner: SEALs of Honor, Book 18

Jackson: SEALs of Honor, Book 19

Kanen: SEALs of Honor, Book 20

Nelson: SEALs of Honor, Book 21

SEALs of Honor, Books 1–3

SEALs of Honor, Books 4–6

SEALs of Honor, Books 7–10

SEALs of Honor, Books 11–13

SEALs of Honor, Books 14–16

SEALs of Honor, Books 17–19

Heroes for Hire

Levi's Legend: Heroes for Hire, Book 1

Stone's Surrender: Heroes for Hire, Book 2

SEALs of Steel

Collections
Dare to Be You…
Dare to Love…
Dare to be Strong…
RomanceX3

Standalone Novellas
It's a Dog's Life
Riana's Revenge
Second Chances

Published Young Adult Books:

Family Blood Ties Series
Vampire in Denial
Vampire in Distress
Vampire in Design
Vampire in Deceit
Vampire in Defiance
Vampire in Conflict
Vampire in Chaos
Vampire in Crisis
Vampire in Control
Vampire in Charge
Family Blood Ties Set 1–3
Family Blood Ties Set 1–5
Family Blood Ties Set 4–6
Family Blood Ties Set 7–9
Sian's Solution, A Family Blood Ties Series Prequel
    Novelette

Design series

Dangerous Designs
Deadly Designs
Darkest Designs
Design Series Trilogy

Standalone

In Cassie's Corner
Gem Stone (a Gemma Stone Mystery)
Time Thieves

Published Non-Fiction Books:

Career Essentials

Career Essentials: The Résumé
Career Essentials: The Cover Letter
Career Essentials: The Interview
Career Essentials: 3 in 1

Made in the USA
Middletown, DE
26 May 2019